the moon is following me

the moon is following me

cecil browne

Matador
5 Weir Road
Kibworth Beauchamp
Leicester LE8 0LQ, UK
Tel: (+44) 116 279 2299
Fax: (+44) 116 279 2277
Email: books@troubador.co.uk
Web: www.troubador.co.uk/matador

ISBN 978 1848762 794

British Library Cataloguing in Publication Data.
A catalogue record for this book is available from the British Library.

Typeset in 11.5pt Sabon MT by Troubador Publishing Ltd, Leicester, UK
Printed and bound in Great Britain by TJ International Ltd, Padstow, Cornwall

Matador is an imprint of Troubador Publishing Ltd

*For my wife and daughters for their support
and encouragement*

*For my niece, Laurie O'Garro, my 'Editor',
for her dedication and integrity*

For Fran Herbert, for careful reading and valuable suggestions

contents

Foreword

The stories in this collection recall the era when the village was the centre of life in the Caribbean island of St Vincent and the Grenadines, SVG. Nostalgic, but not sentimental, they relate the experiences of a range of characters striving to make a name for themselves; they are people in search of a larger stage.

Readers from SVG will note at once that I have taken liberties with the geography of the islands: some of the names of the villages were simply irresistible.

The stories are at times funny and unsettling but, apart from Spanish Ladies, never sad. These are 'real' people, individual, ambitious, mad, vengeful, naïve: they have universal appeal.

the moon is following me

Sans Souci School was without doubt the dullest in the parish of Charlotte; nothing ever happened there.

The school in the adjacent village, Colonarie, had a reputation as a haven for the idle and weird. One of its senior teachers, Parnell Gaymes, was a prosperous banana farmer. A slight man with a mouth permanently ajar, rumour had it that he would change into his farming clothes on the first stroke of twelve, chop bananas furiously for fifty minutes, then don his crisp white shirt and tight black trousers for an afternoon of Geography and Hygiene as though he had simply taken a lunchtime stroll to nearby Grand Sable.

Another teacher, Annis Tannis, a pretty woman with a sad face and a stinking temper, frequently turned up on her boyfriend's Suzuki *after* registration, scowled and barked at Class 4 for three hours, then disappeared for lunch on the Suzuki, never to return for the day. No one knew where she went; she didn't answer to her husband, she had even less time for the headmaster. How Chrissy Black wished that Sans Souci School had such characters; how he wished that someone, pupil or teacher, or some event, would turn it into news.

But in his ten years there, he had experienced nothing but disappointment. Dedicated and hardworking, his teachers were as dull in their personal lives as they were at school. 'Mr Edwards couldn't start a fire in a bakery,' Kenroy Shallow once said of the Science teacher, 'and as for prim Miss Small, if you fling her into Caratal River, her bodice probably wouldn't get wet.'

Only the headmaster, Mr Jackson, had some colour. Too clever for the school and unashamedly fond of rum, he could barely bring himself to speak to the other teachers. Yet, half-sober during the weekly assembly, he never forgot to congratulate a girl who had won a scholarship to a High School, to praise a boy who had scored a century, or to extend his best wishes to a teacher leaving for further study.

The only real excitement came from a stream that trickled past the school on its way through the banana field to the sea a mile away. During the rainy season the pupils prayed that it would overflow its bank and flood the crumbling concrete building.

Once or twice a year their prayers would be answered and they would be sent home for three days until the schoolyard had been cleared of stones, mud, banana stalks and coconut branches, and the classrooms made ready for their return.

Then things would quickly get back to normal, the bell at eight interrupting games of 'In the Pond', cricket, 'corkins' or marbles, the afternoon break adjusted if morning recess overran.

Lunch sent the students rushing home or to the nearby shops and, before you could say, 'Climb a gru-gru tree', there'd be the afternoon lessons of Geography, Science or British History for the seniors and Singing, Hygiene or Caribbean History for the juniors. School-life ambled along like a month of lazy Sundays. Then Betty Laban arrived.

Chrissy can still remember the day she came. It was a scorching Tuesday, the sun stinging bare arms and heads, pupils stepping over dead-eyed sleeping dogs to get to the shop for a cooling drink. The headmaster had managed to rouse himself from his office and was waiting by the road, polite and sober enough to remain upright throughout the three minutes it took to welcome them to Sans Souci.

Chrissy watched a Land Rover pull up at the entrance, a muddy-green vehicle with charcoal-black new tyres. Through a wooden slat at the rear of the classroom he observed two girls descend from the front seat, bright and confident, leather satchels slung diagonally across their cream bodices. There was no need to ask who they were, for the rumours of a new district pharmacist had been rife for weeks. Mr Jackson obviously knew, but it hadn't occurred to Chrissy that they would be attending the local school.

A few days after Betty joined Class 6, he wished that she had gone to the private school five miles away in Chester Cottage, where the well-off parents sent their children.

'Oh good, it's Mathematics next,' she purred as they got out their rulers, 'I do like *Mathematics*, don't you? I don't know why they call it *Arithmetic*.'

Her first week at the school and she had taken up a seat in the middle of the front row, holding court like someone who had been in the class for years.

'Yeah, we like Maths too,' his classmates agreed, lying like horses trotting, 'yeah, Maths nice, you see!'

To Chrissy's consternation, even Brian Best, who struggled with his times tables and was permitted by Mr Jackson to do English during Arithmetic, even he had agreed with her! He watched the deserters from his gang, the traitors, amazed at their defection. How quickly they had latched onto Betty!

It wasn't long before curiosity and quiet admiration turned to dislike. Within months she had 'stolen' his friends. Wherever she went, a small group was close behind, lapping up tales of growing up in Trinidad, Barbados, St Lucia and Dominica. They were in awe of her, this fifteen-year old girl who had been to so many places, who had lived so much, and yet had chosen to be with them at Sans Souci. Exotic, refined, she made them forget Colonarie School.

She had travelled well, Chrissy was forced to admit. Observant beyond her fifteen years, she could bring the countries to life with loving descriptions of the people, food, customs, fashion and music. Her St Lucian patois made Brian laugh until he cried, a Dominican dance shocked them with its delicate simplicity. With a beautifully light Caribbean voice that betrayed no particular island, a quick eye and a passion for detail, even the teachers admired her style and self-confidence.

Where Chrissy had reigned for years he now had a rival. Her algebra equalled his, in History and Geography first-hand experience lent her an advantage over his 'book-learning'. Only in Science did she stumble; her explanation of the cause of the seasons had shamed Mr Edwards into covering his eyes and thumping the desk in frustration.

For sharing with the class the delights of her travels she had a request, she announced to her classmates one Wednesday, so casually that she might have been asking to borrow a pencil. She was asking them to change, she said, simple as that. Change not only how they saw themselves, but also how they thought of themselves. She was going to teach them what her travels had taught her, the value of 'presenting' themselves to the world and of the need to 'talk properly' if they wanted to get on in life.

'Personally, I don't have a problem with the way you talk,' she told Marilyn Green that lunchtime, 'but imagine that you're going for a bank job in Kingstown: you think you'll get it?'

Marilyn was a solid girl, light-complexioned, with light-blue eyes and large, even, white teeth. Well-off and ambitious, she wasn't one to back down.

'Who you talking to, me?' she replied.

'Yes you.'

'Then of course I will get the job. If I had six subjects, how they going to turn me down?'

'They could turn you down even if you had ten subjects.'

'Let them try. Let them try and they will see what will happen!'

'Marilyn, can I give you a bit of advice? Subjects alone won't get you far, understand that. I knew a girl in Barbados who had seven top grades and where did she end up? Working in a store. If you want to get a respectable job when you leave school you have to know how to create an impression, you have to *look* good, you have to *talk* good.'

'Well that was Barbados and this is SVG. I know I look good and I can talk, can't I?'

'There's talk and there's *talk*.'

'What's wrong with the way I talk?'

'Well, I hope you don't get vex or anything, but when you are angry or excited you sound very "country".'

'That is *your* opinion.'

'Maybe. But remember the time Miss Small gave you a *B* for your History homework, you remember how you curse and swear like a market woman?'

'We can't all be like you, Miss Proper.'

'I'm happy with the way I am.'

'And so am I, TYVM.'

'TYVM?'

'Thank You Very Much!'

With this Marilyn had turned her back on Betty and marched off to the shop across the road swearing under her breath.

But Betty wasn't discouraged.

> *The thundering train that flashes by*
> *Is but a dark speck against the vast blue sky.*

She tried to make some of her classmates recite this one afternoon after a game of rounders.

'Wonderful lines, aren't they?' she suggested. 'They're from a poem I studied in Trinidad. Try saying them out loud, try it. Simply let the words trip off the tongue.'

Ada Grace had a go, Elfredo Wilkins tried, and finally, in an effort to please her, Martha Joseph.

'This is stupidness,' Osmond Green told her, refusing point blank to try, 'I can't read such foolishness. Besides, trains don't thunder, trains glide.'

The problem was simple: none of them had ever seen a real train. Like the westerns they clambered over one another to see at the cinema in Georgetown at Sunday matinees, trains and horses belonged to the world of movies or to the larger Caribbean islands, Trinidad, Jamaica and Cuba.

'You might as well ask us to describe a day in winter,' Chrissy said, to explain their difficulty, 'we've never seen snow, we've never felt the cold, where do we begin?'

'Imagination, Chrissy!' Betty retorted, 'that's what English is about, isn't it?'

'I know, but some things are just too difficult.'

'It's the same as writing about electricity in Science: you close your eyes and use your imagination: unless that was *your* imagination I passed going down the road this morning.'

After that incident Chrissy decided to keep his distance: she could have the battle. He began to sit at the back of the class with the boys who didn't care for cleverness in girls but were more interested in their legs and developing breasts, and who were left alone provided they weren't too disruptive and kept out of the teachers' way. Michael Wilson and Ian Stapleton became his new friends. To eighteen-year old Michael who had finished school the previous year but who still insisted on coming despite being banned by Mr Jackson, Betty was 'Not bad: yes, she quite good-looking.'

'She could walk, you see,' Ian casually observed as they watched her going to the shop one lunchtime, 'she languid, that girl have real motion.'

Chrissy didn't know about any of those things. She had full, brown eyes, alert and bright, and with more than a hint of mischief, he knew, and thick eyebrows. Neat and wonderfully symmetrical, her face was uniformly black. Through her billowing white bodice her slowly-maturing figure was obvious. And such delicate fingers! In a Science lesson, as she struggled to point to a *line of latitude* on a globe, he had seen them uncertain for the first time.

But he wasn't interested in her walk, her figure, her slender fingers or her eyes: she had lured away his friends, she looked down on him, she had vowed to change them as though they were children: he hated girls like her.

Three months later, the class had a Geography trip to Peter's Hope, a popular beach on the leeward coast. Chrissy had expected her to decline the trip. She wasn't the type to mix out of school, he had decided, their casual conversation would be beneath a girl of her sensitivity. An hour of Michael's coarse jokes in the van was bound to embarrass her, and the idea of sixteen pupils crammed into a van licensed for ten would surely keep her at home. But there she was at eight, basket overflowing like a trader at Lowmans market, greeting everyone, at ease in the company of her classmates and teachers. Chrissy's heart sank. That girl, that girl!

She was everywhere, there was no escaping her. In the playground, at the shop where the pupils gathered, as he walked along the banks of the stream on the way home from school she appeared in his mind, smiling, waving, full of life, a girl untouched by the worries of the world. At breakfast he heard her voice, soft, a whisper, asking for his help in Science, or full of confidence, requesting that they compare answers in Maths. Betty Laban, that girl, that girl!

On the journey to Peter's Hope he sat at the back of the van with Michael and Ian who only came to school for the girls or during the sports season, or for free outings such as that one. He didn't swim when the others did, he ate his breadfruit and stewed saltfish at eleven in the shade of a high rock when Michael and Ian were diving for jacks they had no chance of spearing with homemade fish-guns.

At midday, as he was sheltering from the heat, he could hear light footsteps on the dry grape leaves. Rubbing away the beginnings of sleep from his eyes, he yawned and sat up. As he stretched and gathered himself he found Betty standing over him, basket in hand, like a vendor. She smiled as he brushed the white sand from his hair and bare back, as though she had caught him undressing.

'What's the matter, Chrissy, sun too hot for you?' she asked, with a grin he didn't care for.

'Just cooling off,' he replied in the most casual manner he could summon, 'just getting ready to go fishing.'

'You look like you could use a drink. Want some soursop juice?'

'I'm not thirsty.'

'Go on, try it. It's got nutmeg, cloves and cinnamon. I got the recipe in Grenada. It's really nice.'

'I just had some sorrel.'

'I've got some tamarind balls in the basket, would you like one?'

'No.'

'Go on, take one.'

'I'm not hungry.'

'Fine, Chrissy, you think I care?' She took a sip of the soursop juice and bit into a tamarind ball as if to convince him that they weren't poisoned. 'You have a problem, boy, a real problem.'

'I don't have a problem, thank you very much. I can't stand soursop, and tamarind can stay on the tree and it wouldn't bother me.'

'Fine. Fine, Chrissy Black, fine.'

'Fine yourself. Go and meet your friends: I have fish to catch.'

As he changed to go swimming, he could see her in the distance sharing soursop juice, tamarind balls and coconut tarts to their classmates. Their cackling, like children who have just discovered a new naughty word, floated to him on the warm sea breeze. She was really getting under his skin.

The trip was uneventful but Class 6 had expected that. Miss Small read a romantic novel under a coconut tree while Mr Edwards studied a science journal behind trendy sunglasses. Forced to remain sober because he was the driver, Mr Jackson, a ghost in green swimming trunks, stared at the sea as though he expected a monster to emerge from the blue depths and devour them all.

Back from his swim Chrissy watched them and imagined a similar outing with the teachers of Colonarie School. He could visualise Parnell Gaymes and Annis Tannis swimming out to where only their heads were visible from land, or taking their lunch in one of the boats anchored far out at sea. Their meal of lobster and pelau, out at sea, or on the beach in full view of the pupils, would be washed down with beer or a small rum, he felt sure.

Left to entertain themselves, the Sans Souci pupils admired the foggy peaks of La Soufriere volcano towering above them, dormant for half a century, magnificent in its sleep. When they tired of this, or of the warm sea, they played rounders and dodgeball on the beach or raced along the hot sand. As the teachers slept, the pupils chased crabs or picked grapes.

'A lovely day out, wasn't it Class 6?' Miss Small asked on Monday, 'everyone had a good time, didn't they?'

Any Friday away from school was a good Friday, Chrissy thought of saying what most of the class felt, but instead he joined the chorus and answered, 'Yes Miss, it was a wonderful trip.'

'Well, children,' Miss Small continued, 'I hope you've all prepared a story or a drawing, something educational, to mark the visit.'

Knowing Miss Small's method, Ian had prepared a sketch of Peters Hope from the main road, hundreds of erect coconut trees trapping the light, and Chrissy had collected eleven pebbles for a talk about volcanoes.

'Miss Small,' it was Betty, 'Miss Small?'

'Yes, Betty?'

'Can I do mine now, please? I won't be in tomorrow or Thursday, I have to go Kingstown with Mother.'

'You mean your piece is ready?'

'Yes, Miss Small.'

'All right then, let's hear your offering.'

Ian's sketches had to wait, Chrissy's pebbles, rough with specks of glittering mineral or smoothed by the action of the waves over decades, remained in their bag on the floor next to his chair. Armed with five sheets of paper, Betty waltzed to the front of the class.

A slight cough to clear her throat, then she began.

We left the moon in Peter's Hope
To go back to Sans Souci
The stars were out, the clouds had gone
The night was in its infancy

As we got to Kingstown
I chanced to look above
The golden moon was still there
Like a faithful love

At Villa I was growing tired
The long day taking its toll
The moon I so admired
Glowing, shiny, getting more bold

What, I asked at Belle Vue
Just what on earth could it be?
I thought I'd left the moon behind
But still it was there with me!

Home we drove, exhausted
At last we were in Sans Souci
I looked outside and would you believe?
The damn moon was still following me!

Betty bowed expansively, shuffled the sheets, then slowly made her way back to her seat. Not knowing what to make of what he had heard, Chrissy felt as awkward as Betty looked when the expected applause didn't arrive. Solid naked black arms akimbo, Miss Small gave Betty a severe 'bad eye', like a girl embarrassed by her younger sister cartwheeling and revealing her underwear in public.

'Thank you Betty,' she said sternly, 'thanks for your lovely *poem*.'

Several pupils tittered and Marilyn burst out laughing.

'The moon following me,' she said scornfully, 'you ever hear such nonsense?'

At that moment the bell went for morning recess and the pupils piled out into the schoolyard. Betty and Chrissy remained in the classroom.

'You like my present?' she asked.

'What present?' he replied.

'My poem: You like it?'

'No.'

'And I stayed up half the night to finish it?'

'You should have gone to bed early.'

'Why, what's wrong with it?'

'If you don't know, I'm not going to tell you.'

'It wasn't *that* bad, was it?'

'Go and ask Marilyn.'

'It took me an hour to write.'

'You mean ten minutes?'

'Honest, it took an hour.'

'If you say so.'

'Never mind, it wasn't meant for you anyway. It was for the rest of the class. It's my leaving present.'

'Your what?'

'My goodbye present.'

'But you can't leave!'

'I can.'

'But why?'

'It's not my decision: mother's off again. This place is no good for the business. The medicines not selling, she's losing money. She says it looks like people in SVG don't get sick.'

'So you have to go?'

'Yes, we're on the move again. Trinidad, Barbados, Grenada, St Lucia, Dominica and now St Vincent: at this rate we'll be up to Cuba by the time I'm seventeen.'

A month later, Betty came to the school to say goodbye. They were leaving at the weekend and Chrissy was due to go to Canada.

'A little bird told me you're off, too,' she began as they sat in their classroom.

'Yes, I'm going to Canada to join my parents.'

'Looking forward to it?'

He wasn't excited about leaving but he knew that staying wasn't an option.

'When you have to go you have to go,' he said, repeating one of his father's favourite sayings, 'it might turn out good, it might turn out bad, who knows?'

'We're going to try our luck in Antigua.'

'You're lucky, you know, it must be so exciting taking in so many different islands.'

'It's not as exciting as you think. You go to a place, you make new friends and just when you're really getting to know them, you have to start all over again.'

'You'll be all right, you make friends easily.'

'Do I?'

'Yes, you had the whole class with you here.'

Her thick black hair was neatly parted down the middle; two fat plaits ran backwards, converging at the back of her neck. Red and veiny, as though she had spent the morning in the sea, her eyes sat unhappily in the young, pretty, black face. It was the first time he had seen her looking sad and lonely.

'I don't know about that,' she said finally, as though she couldn't think of what else to say, 'I get the feeling some people didn't like me.'

'You're wrong, you were the most popular person in the class. And it will be the same in Antigua.'

'You'll do well in Canada too. Just don't forget the friends you left behind.'

'You mean Ian and Michael?'

'And others.'

'Like who?'

'Me.'

'You? You're my friend?'

'Of course I am.'

'I didn't know that.'

'Then you have a lot to learn.'

'And who's going to teach me?'

'I could have taught you. But some other girl will, don't worry. Some other girl will take my place.'

She had been sitting by the door; she came and sat beside him. Chrissy thought of taking her hand and stroking her fingers. Instead he took her by the shoulders and drew her to him. He could feel her young heart racing, although it could have been his.

He kissed her.

After a minute or so she eased her body away from his.

'I have to go, they're waiting for me outside.'

'Who?'

'Father and my sister. Mother's gone to say goodbye to Mr Jackson.'

Chrissy took her left hand and squeezed her forearm hard. Ignoring her grimace he squeezed her a second time. He wanted to hurt her for leaving.

'You won't forget me, will you?' she said, as she released herself from his grip.

Betty walked slowly away. Chrissy watched her go and wondered why life was so unfair, why it sometimes takes away before we could properly understand.

At the classroom door Betty turned, smiled and waved.

'Don't worry, Betty,' he said as she opened the door to go, ' I'll never forget you.'

take for two

Poor Archie, so much trouble! An expensive wedding dress all the way from America and no bride to wear it!

Archie was from Happy Hill. At age eleven, an argument with his uncle about the parrot he kept in his bedroom had forced him to leave. After wandering for two days he had found himself in Chauncey.

Few could remember his arrival. Norman Moses, the self-appointed 'eyes of the village', could recall him ordering a fruit cocktail at the gas station at Questelles and Sammy Jessop heard him asking directions to Belair. For the rest he might well have grown up in Chauncey. So completely had he taken to the village that whenever he was asked where he was from he would answer roughly, 'Chauncey nuh!'

The sea was life in his new home. The village boasted that its children could swim and fish before they could walk. Archie didn't care for fishing. The sea water reddened his eyes and left his skin coarse, dry and white, the salt lingered in his mouth for days. He preferred to work on the roads, fixing the gutters or mending potholes. For the frail old women and men of the village, he cleared their yard of weeds and white snakes. No task was below him, he worked slowly but solidly.

Punctual and reliable, he was seldom without a job. But he wanted more than toiling in the hot sun all day and going home to an ungrateful parrot or a pack of cards. With dreams of a grander home, when he was nineteen, Archie joined up to go to America to pick apples.

Fitzroy John and Dennis Ribeiro had gone the year before and returned full of tales and brimming with 'real money'. Every day for an entire week, Dennis had produced a bulging wallet of crisp notes and allowed his close friends the privilege of sniffing and counting them in *Alfie's Bar*.

More modest and less ostentatious, Fitzroy had bought drinks for the men on the first night back, then faded into his regular job at sea in Clare Valley and Camden Park. Archie wanted some of the American action; he wanted a name in the village; the time had come for half-naked children to stop asking where he was from.

Stocky for five-feet seven, handsome, with small ears and curled lips, Fitzroy John was a saver. Archie used to watch him and Dennis carefully, noting their mannerisms as though they were his rivals at cards. They were so different, one all smiles and laughter, the other quiet, contemplative like the fisherman he was.

Dennis hated quiet. Over six feet, brown-black, loud, with long muscular arms, you couldn't help noticing him. 'Make it, spend it!' he boasted when he was entertaining his friends with rum, whisky and fried fish every Friday evening, 'so I make money, so I spend money. You can't take it with you so why hang on to it?' Dennis didn't know it but he was Archie's hero; whatever he did Archie vowed silently to emulate.

The tales of the American experience captivated Archie. Those delicious nights gambling and drinking until four only to be awoken soon after to be driven to the orchard: now that was real living! As he played cards in his one-room house, a restless parrot watching his every move, he pictured himself in a spacious smoke-filled bar with Dennis and Fitzroy, not at the centre of things, but close enough to the action to count as one of the men.

Weekends of rum and whisky, women of all nationalities bussed in on Saturday nights to 'entertain', the arguments and scuffles between men forced to bunk in tiny dormitories like schoolboys or scouts: Archie couldn't wait to be part of it all. But his dream was about to come true, he was going to 'do America'. And with thousands of dollars to bank when he returned, who could fail to notice him?

'When I was a young boy,' Dennis loved to boast to Archie when nostalgic with rum, 'when I was young, Chauncey people had class. The women knew how to dress, they could hold a conversation on any topic. But most of all they could move!'

'How you mean?'

'Move nuh! You don't know how women does move?'

'I suppose so.'

'I used to sit all day watching them go about their business and wonder who teach them how to carry their body.'

'For truth?'

'For truth. Those were the days Archie boy, those days could never come again. Karen John, Sita Pilgrim, Estelle Black, Mavis George and Elsie Pompey, the amount of marriage proposals they used to get from big-shot businessmen in Kingstown!'

'Those old women?'

'Those same old women who end up teaching and nursing and raising family. When I was a young man, if they look at me and smile, I was happy for the rest of the day!'

'Murder!'

'The men them were grand too, you know. Especially those who used to work in the oil refinery in Curacao or the salt mines in Aruba. They did themselves and the village proud. Big men they were, Archie, big, big men. Old Bascombe, Mr Glasgow, Pico and Billingy, they in their eighties and shaky now, but the night Bascombe return from Aruba the whole village catch fire. You should have been there, Archie boy. Music play through the night, nobody sleep. Two taxis from Kingstown it take to bring him home. Two brand new vehicles. The first one pull up in front of his house, he climb out like he is royalty and start to share out money, dollar bills for the adults, coins for the children. While he hugging and kissing everyone, the driver have to ask for help to unload seven suitcases they so heavy. Good old Bascombe! Five minutes later a second taxi turn up. Only this one empty! Except for Bascombe black felt hat perch on the back seat!'

Archie loved to hear this story. Dennis told it almost every Friday when the men gathered at his house or at *Alfie's*, yet he laughed like a stranger hearing it for the first time. He wanted some of that fame. He wanted to be accepted in the village; he wanted to bury Happy Hill.

A month before the men were due to depart Archie took a van to Kingstown to order some trousers for the trip. Young and fit as he was, it was best not to take chances. The cold evenings and frosty mornings on the orchard would find him well prepared.

Two made-to-measure khaki trousers for work and a third for casual wear were just the thing, he had decided. Khaki was the standard for the men of the village, it made them look good, it gave them confidence. Strong and comfortable, it had served Dennis and Fitzroy well in America and he was sure it wouldn't let him down when his turn came. With the self-importance of a first-time traveller he had the tailor take his measurements twice. Before paying the fifteen-dollars deposit he checked the entries against his name four times. 'Two weeks,' he reminded the tailor as he left the shop, 'don't forget: two weeks.' His business in town concluded, he bought two loaves of bread and a bag of cakes at the market and caught the next van home.

As the van stopped to pick up a passenger at the gas station at Questelles, he awoke from a cat nap. Travelling in a van always had that effect on him. 'By the gap,' he said sleepily when he realised where he was, 'by the next gap.' Always a man for a quick getaway he got out his fare, five dollars, from his back pocket, and steadied himself to relay it via two passengers to the conductor. But the van braked suddenly, causing him to repocket his money.

The left side door slid open as the van came to rest at the turning for Chauncey. Four passengers got out and, from the back seat, Archie followed, feeling for his wallet as he stepped onto firm ground. Ruthlyn Guilding, a neighbour, was at the front of the queue to pay the conductor. Money in hand, the passengers waited. Ruthlyn shook her purse vigorously, twisting it this way then that to dislodge the coins. The wait increased. Anxious and frustrated, picking out one coin at a time and placing it in the conductor's outstretched palm like a child learning to count, she apologised to the passengers behind her.

'Sorry, but I don't know where the money gone. Three-twenty, three dollars thirty, three fifty-five, wait, let me see, I have a dollar in here somewhere.'

'Take for two,' Archie said to the conductor, stepping forward and passing over a ten-dollar note, 'take for two.'

If you sleep in Chauncey someone will notice you when you wake up; a new baby is christened by the villagers before its parents could agree a name. So when, at five o'clock, as he was buying some sardines to go with the bread for his supper, he heard someone call out, 'Take for two!', Archie wasn't totally surprised. Later that evening, as he sat in the porch watching the night deepen, two little girls went past. 'Good evening,' said the first politely, 'Take for two,' said the second with a giggle. Before he could spring to his feet to identify them they had scampered off into the night.

Those who didn't have anything better to do revelled in that sort of thing, he said to himself, at first annoyed, then, as the realisation dawned on him, with a growing feeling of satisfaction. He was being noticed. Adults had re-christened him, children teased him like they teased Pico about his wooden leg. What was wrong with two of them having a little girlish fun?

As the name solidified he found himself at Ruthlyn's house. The villagers expected it, it seemed as natural as rain in August. And she didn't seem to mind.

On Sunday, taking a morning stroll, he nodded and said hello.

The following day they talked for two minutes, Ruthlyn apologising and promising to repay the fare, Archie refusing to accept her money. Rare turpentine mangoes were his first gift to her, two pounds of snapper following swiftly when he saw the look of appreciation in her face.

Sweeping the yard, watering the flowers and plants in their garden, she seemed to spend more time outside the house she shared with her mother and younger sister. Archie took this as a signal that she was interested. He watched her lovingly as she hung out the washing, he noted each trip to the shop. When she went swimming at Indian Bay with her sister, he waited patiently in the porch for them to return.

A year older than he was, twenty, with a high forehead and near-perfect, black skin, Ruthlyn worked as a receptionist in Kingstown. She was thin, with a narrow face and cheekbones that accentuated the narrowness. Good-looking, but not striking, Archie would gaze at her cherry-black lips and imagine his first kiss.

Comfortable in the company of the men of the village he had never had much interest in women. Yet he began to notice the skirt dancing about Ruthlyn's knees, the plaits she favoured, the arch of her eyebrows, and the perfume she wore to work. In the evening with his deck of cards he imagined the two of them playing 'Twenty-one' or 'Snap', touching hands in childish haste to play the winner. Dennis, Fitzroy, Bascombe and Mr Glasgow, Sita Pilgrim and the women from the thirties who had so enthralled Dennis gradually lost their attraction. In his eyes Ruthlyn was their equal.

The week he was due to leave she cooked him a meal, a fish

broth steaming with onions and black pepper. Archie didn't like fish, and he didn't care for 'hot' food. But he thanked her sincerely, ate even the bones, and then they reverted to the awkwardness that was their relationship.

There were so many things to say to her but he didn't have the words; and although she didn't say directly that she looked forward to his visits, he felt that she did. They had become a habit. Thrown together by gossip and rumour, their evenings together in the porch were enjoyable. In their own way they were happy together. When he attempted a joke she smiled, a clumsy attempt to kiss her goodnight one Sunday had made her chuckle.

Yet she was so undemonstrative, Archie would reflect when alone with his cards, she asked so little of him. An hour would pass with them sitting side by side, backs to the road, and at the end of it she would fidget with the hem of her dress or gather her shoes, and he would take it as a sign that it was getting late.

The following night she would smile sweetly to welcome him, ask about his day and talk about hers. For the rest of the time conversation would be difficult. Archie blamed her shyness and his lack of experience with women. But there was no hurry, he told himself, the talking would come in time: he would find the words and she would know how to respond.

The night before he left for America he went to the house.

'Well, Ruthlyn, I'm off soon.'

'Yes, I know.'

'This time tomorrow, I'm sleeping in America.'

'Yes.'

'I'm really looking forward to it, you know.'

'You don't have to tell me that.'

'Dennis say is the best thing that happen to him.'

'Dennis have too much talk.'

'I'm going to work hard and save my money. When I come back I'm going to set myself up.'

'Good for you Archie.'

'I can't wait, I wish today was tomorrow.'

'You mustn't rush time.'

'I'm not rushing time: I'm dying to go and earn some real cash and then come back to Chauncey and settle down.'

'Take your time Archie, savour the experience, enjoy yourself.'

'With Dennis and Fitzroy for company I can't go wrong.'

'If you say so.'

'What you want me get you? What you want me bring you back?'

'Nothing, you don't have to get me anything.'

'But I want to get you something.'

'You don't have to.'

'You think I'm going to go all that way and come back empty-handed like I just pop up to Georgetown for the day or van into Kingstown to pay the light bill? No, tell me what you want.'

'Well, a dress. Get me a dress.'

'What kind of dress?'

'You're a man, aren't you? Surprise me! Get me a dress, a special dress.'

A goodbye kiss on her cheek and Archie departed into the night full of hope.

The first week in America Archie worked and slept, slept and worked. Picking apples wasn't demanding but the hours drained even the strongest men. By the third week, however, he considered himself fully settled. He could keep up with the fittest men in his dormitory, he had adjusted to the light and the weather. He was ready for action. Bring on the fun, he said, let the entertainment begin.

But most of the men were too tired to quarrel; a fight would have been as surprising as a hurricane in February. The nightly cooks, the card-playing and drinking Dennis used to boast about must be taking place in one of the adjacent dormitories, he concluded, for the majority of the men in his took to their bunks directly after their evening meal at eight. The Dennis of *Alfie's Bar*, energetic, vivacious, unstoppable, was too worn out for conversation until Friday evening.

But Archie didn't mind; he was accustomed to his own company. Besides, he told himself, every card game missed was a saving, each bottle of whisky that remained on the shelf boosted his account by a few dollars. Only at the weekend when the women arrived at the compound did he feel slightly homesick.

Satisfied that he could last the contract, he phoned Ruthlyn to share the news. She wasn't at home, her mother answered, she was working late.

A fortnight passed. He phoned again. She was spending the weekend with her aunt in Belvedere, her mother apologised again, he should try on Monday, she would definitely be in then.

Archie became anxious. Where was she, why didn't she come to the phone, didn't she know how he felt about her? In his dreams he saw her sitting in the porch reading a newspaper or book, his chair empty beside hers. As they drove to work in the morning, while the other men slept, he would take out a picture of Ruthlyn her nine-year old sister had stolen for him for a dollar and gaze at it until the face in the photograph broke into a smile. He missed their evenings together, he missed their silence.

To take his mind off her, he started a fitness routine. Younger than most of the men, he waited until they were asleep and did hundreds of press-ups and sit-ups. Up early, he repeated the regime, adding stretching and twisting. But that wasn't enough, another distraction was needed: he decided to grow a beard. Training drove away his worries, the beard gave him something to look forward to each morning.

'Don't worry,' Dennis advised, when he mentioned his concern one evening when they were alone, 'Ruthlyn's fine.'

'How you know that?'

'Trust me.'

'Trust you?'

'Yes, my wife said so in a letter.'

'She said that? She said Ruthlyn fine?'

'Well, not exactly.'

'Well what then?'

'She said that Chauncey was as quiet as a Sunday, that even Norman Moses was struggling to dig up a little gossip or scandal.'

'You sure?'

'Sure I sure.'

The news pleased Archie. Chauncey was quiet, Ruthlyn was well. In his absence she was probably visiting relatives or working late to occupy herself.

Two weeks before the end of the contract Archie decided to buy the dress. He had been planning to get it but couldn't risk the other men finding out. A friend of Fitzroy's had a reputation as a 'fingersmith' and Archie's suitcase had a single lock: the thought of someone discovering the dress and parading it before the other men was one Archie dreaded more than anything in the world. Big news on the compound, the newspapers and radio back at home would burn for a week. Buying the dress early was risky, but with home looming, Archie had to act.

'A dress, a special dress': Archie saw this as his mission. The savings he had accumulated were fine but the dress would crown the trip. He imagined the girlish delight on Ruthlyn's face, saw her speechless when presented with the foreign gift.

A mall on the route to the orchard looked promising. Only five miles from the compound, the moment the automatic doors let him through he felt a lightness in his heart. He was only minutes from his special purchase, Ruthlyn was going to be the happiest woman in Chauncey!

But ignorant of her tastes or dress size, he struggled at first to explain fully his wishes. He had seen her dressed for work and in casual clothes but he couldn't recall her dressed for a special occasion. Muttering to himself at his ignorance of women, he thought hard, screwed up his face, stroked his beard and pointed to various designs in the catalogue.

'I don't mean to intrude,' the owner of the boutique said, 'but it's unusual for a man to make this type of purchase.'

Archie grunted.

'Sir, a wedding dress is like no other dress: design, style, touch, texture, stitching, shades of colour are so important and individual, women normally take a month, if not more, to weigh up the options. It's not unusual for a woman to change her mind several times, to try on every single dress on offer, then try them again in reverse order. Your partner must have absolute faith in you to trust you with such a momentous purchase.'

'We together since we at school.'

'Even so, Sir, this isn't a party dress, this is *the big* one.'

'I know, but we discuss the dress in great detail, the shade, the material and the make. She even draw a picture for me. I know her taste, she trust me.'

Although not fully convinced, the owner persuaded an assistant to try on three different styles for Archie's benefit. Twirling and swaying gently as he suggested, the assistant worked for her money that day.

'Well, sir, which would it be?' asked the owner.

'Number two,' Archie replied, replacing, in his mind, the assistant's full curves with Ruthlyn's straight up and down figure. 'Dress number two is the one.'

'Are you sure, sir?'

'One hundred percent sure. Wrap it up. *Carefully.*'

He paid and hurried home to lock it away at the bottom of his case.

The night they arrived home Archie thought of going straight to Ruthlyn's house. The torment was over. He was desperate to see her, to say that he was back, and confess that he had missed her.

But he knew it wouldn't be the right thing to do. Haste was likely to backfire, he felt instinctively, it was better to wait. Dennis and Fitzroy normally spent the first night regaling the men; his rightful place was there with them.

At seven he joined his friends at the other end of the village for the traditional welcome back. They drank, they boasted, they told tall tales. They laughed, embellished, lied, and laughed even louder. Alfie closed the bar at three in the morning when he ran out of rum, beer, sardines, tarts, drops, bread and cheese. Fearing there'd be nothing but biscuits, butter and sugar to sell for breakfast, he drove the men home to their families.

The following day Archie was up at eleven. Feeling pleased that at last he had joined the men, that he had 'done America', he wandered about the village greeting everyone, shaking hands and receiving congratulations. 'Take for two,' he expected to hear, but the name seemed to have been lost. Even children looking for an opportunity for adult friendship appeared to have forgotten the nickname. But he wasn't too concerned: he was going to see Ruthlyn later that day, why worry about a stupid nickname?

He delayed the visit until he could bear it no longer. At six it was still light, not a good hour for such delicate business. And he couldn't call much after eight because that would be too late. He went at seven-forty.

Ruthlyn's mother welcomed him back and asked how he was. 'Ruthlyn,' she then yelled, 'Archie here.' She nodded for him to enter the house, excused herself, and Archie watched her disappear in the direction of *Alfie's Bar*.

Archie entered. This was his first time in the house itself. A smell of burning candles and *Vicks* greeted him, and the atmosphere was hot and sticky, as though the house hadn't been aired for the day. His heart racing, he stroked the triangular beard of which he had grown quite proud, as he waited. Ruthlyn appeared from a bedroom a few moments later as he was standing awkwardly by the dining table.

'Archie,' she said, as though he had surprised her.

'Ruthlyn.'

'You back.'

'Yes, I came back last night.'

'So I hear. How things, how are you?'

'Things fine. Is good to be home.'

Then, noticing him still standing she said, 'Take a seat Archie, take a seat.'

Archie sat and she joined him at the table.

'How was America?'

'The work wasn't too hard but you had to wake up at five some mornings.'

'But you came through it.'

'Yes.'

'I'm glad.'

'What about you? I phone five-six-seven-eight times but they always say you working.'

Ruthlyn leaned forward, covered her eyes with her left hand, and breathed out loudly.

'Archie,' she said.

'Yes?'

Her face covered with both hands, she began to sob.

'Archie, I'm sorry,' she said, ' really sorry.'

She sobbed for two minutes, face down on the table. Then she got up, wiped away the tears with the back of her right hand and dragged herself back to the bedroom. Archie sat there for a minute or so then, when he realised from the silence in the bedroom that she wasn't coming back, he left.

The next day her sister came with a message for Archie:

Ruthlyn wished to see him. Archie unlocked the suitcase and took out the dress. He waited until he saw her mother and sister going for their daily walk then went over.

He sat in the same chair as the day before and called out in the direction of the bedroom.

Ruthlyn came straight away and sat at the table. Archie hadn't noticed her properly the previous night but now he saw that her face had grown rounder and her figure fuller.

'Archie,' she began.

'Ruthlyn.'

'Archie, I have something to tell you.'

'Yes?'

'Archie, when you was in America.'

'Yes?'

'Archie, when you was in America something happen.'

'What happen?'

'Archie, I'm making a baby.'

Archie couldn't remember how and when he got home that night. Although he lived a few houses away, it was like one of those drunken nights at *Alfie's Bar* when he would find himself in his pyjamas and wonder who had taken him home and dressed him for bed. A baby, he kept saying to himself, Ruthlyn is making a baby! He locked the dress away and, after tossing and turning for over an hour, he eventually fell asleep.

The following evening he confronted Ruthlyn in the road. He had waited for her as she returned from work and, luckily, there was no one about as they walked up the hill to the village.

'Who you making baby for?' Archie asked, getting straight to the point.

Ruthlyn didn't answer.

'What happen, Ruthlyn, you lost your tongue?'

'No.'

'Then why you don't answer: who you making baby for?'

'Nobody.'

'Nobody?'

'Nobody you know.'

'I working like a jackass for you and all the time you going behind my back with Nobody.'

'Archie, me and you was never like that.'

'No?'

'No.'

'Don't tell me, I was just your *friend*, right?'

'Yes: if you want to put it like that.'

'Just your friend? And you had me coming round every night. You had me bringing you presents, you cooking me dinner and things like that and I was only a friend! You let me kiss you and I didn't mean anything to you?'

'Archie I only cook you dinner the once. You was going away and I just feel I had to do something after all the things you do for me. It was just a way of saying thank you and wishing you all the best for the trip. As for the kiss, well, it's what people do when someone going on their travels.'

'And the dress, why you ask me to buy you a "special dress"?'

'Because you force me. I didn't ask for anything but you force me.'

'I didn't force you.'

'You did. You pressurise me.'

Perhaps she was right, he said to himself on reflection,

perhaps he had insisted despite her protests.

'You could keep it anyway,' he said after a moment, ' I don't have any use for it.'

Archie produced the parcel from the bag and said, 'Open it, Ruthlyn, open it.'

'No, Archie, I can't.'

'Open it, I buy it for you.'

'No, I don't want it. I can't take anything from you. It wouldn't be right.'

'All that trouble. All that embarrassment: you think it was easy for me to go into a shop and buy a wedding dress? You think it was easy?'

'Archie, I didn't say anything about wedding dress, I said a special dress.'

'So what kind of dress was you expecting?'

'A simple dress, but nice, special: something to wear to church or a christening or a dance. Something from overseas, something you can't buy in Kingstown.'

'So what I going to do with a wedding dress? What you want me do with it?'

'I don't know Archie, but I can't take it. I don't deserve it.'

'You do. Even after what you do to me, you can still have it.'

Archie forced the parcel into her hand and wandered off in the direction of Questelles.

The following day he locked up his house and left for Happy Hill. Chauncey wasn't really his kind of place after all, he decided. They had never truly accepted him. Despite his years there, he was still an outsider. He would sell the parrot, make up with his uncle and start afresh.

Two weeks later he was back in Chauncey. What had he done to be ashamed of? Nothing. Who had he robbed? Nobody. He hadn't 'bad-talked' man or woman, he didn't beg, he didn't steal. All he possessed he had worked for, the house he lived in he had built with his own money. No one was going to drive him away.

The parcel was in his bedroom waiting for him, with a sealed letter on top. 'Archie, I didn't know you feel that way about me,' the letter began, 'you should have told me, then what happen might not have happen.'

Archie didn't read further. The money from his trip was sitting pretty in the bank, he had his friends, Dennis and Fitzroy, three jobs were waiting for him when he was ready: why bother about a stupid wedding dress?

But now he prayed that the fame he had so desperately sought wouldn't come: a word from Ruthlyn and he was finished in the village. The news might even hit Happy Hill, Clare Valley and Layou and he would have no choice but to go and live somewhere far away on the windward side of the island where no one knew him. He no longer wanted to be popular. Bascombe, Mr Glasgow, Mr Ribeiro, Estelle Black and Sita Pilgrim could keep their place in everyone's memory. A peaceful life was all he wished for now.

Three years after the trip Ruthlyn had still kept their secret. Archie liked that. In a village of rumours, where Norman Moses saw and heard everything, no one knew about the dress. How could he not respect Ruthlyn? And the longer she kept the secret the more his admiration grew.

The child 'agreed' with her, Archie couldn't help noticing, the child had made her blossom. Her face had kept its roundness, the straightness of her figure had been ironed out. And whenever she cooked a particularly good meal, fish broth or peas soup, she would send her sister for him and they would sit at the dining table, eat, joke and talk like best friends. 'Take for two', a passer-by would occasionally hail him as he and Ruthlyn sat in the porch, their backs to the road. 'Aaaaaay,' he would acknowledge the caller with a wave of the right hand, 'right-right.'

A shy boy, her son loved to play with the tennis balls Archie bought him. The boy came to his house to play with the parrot every day and on Sundays they went swimming in the sea at Shipping Bay. Ruthlyn sometimes joined them, walking along the hot black sand and throwing pebbles at some imaginary target in the sea as they swam. Some day, Archie felt sure, some day Ruthlyn would come to him to reclaim the dress.

He had time, he was prepared to wait.

spanish ladies

Ralph Emmanuel and I left Stinking Tree Village Primary School in St Vincent and the Grenadines in 1965. The reward for our nine years at the school was a *School-Leaving Certificate* and the faint hope of a place at Stubbs Secondary, five miles away.

A transfer to Stubbs Secondary promised much. The head took in pupils at fifteen or even sixteen, as long as they could pay for their own textbooks and transport, or if they were good at sports.

At that age, trim and fit, five miles was no distance for me. With the money I had saved, textbooks weren't a problem either. But over the long July-August holidays I lost interest and ended up submitting the application form late. I had genuinely wanted to go to secondary school, but Ralph wasn't particularly bothered. He had had enough of school, teachers, studying and getting up early only to be bossed around, and I convinced myself that I, too, deserved a change.

I was probably his only friend at the time for he wasn't very talkative. He would sit with the boys in Elnora Seaton's yard for an hour, smile at the lewd songs and jokes but remain on the edge of things. Teasing him about his father's poor hygiene drew a shrug of the shoulders. Those who suggested that his sister wore her skirts too short wasted their time. Quiet though he was, and hard to provoke, I sensed that he wanted a friend, and I was happy to drift with anyone who didn't get into serious trouble.

Two months later, on the first Monday in September, as we watched the new crop of pupils scurry from the village, we looked at one another and shrugged our shoulders. For we knew we would have to take whatever came along or join the boys who went from village to village, spending a month with relatives or friends before moving on. Work being seasonal, our days would consist of fishing at Black Point and cooking our catch on the beach, or watching the girls come and go from home to shop or school, in the hope that one day they might notice us.

Ralph was very tall, with round shoulders and a long, slim neck. Sixteen, a month older than me, his round black face seldom managed more than a smile. He was good at History and Science but, like me, he hadn't planned beyond leaving school. After our rejection from Stubbs – 'too old, too late, but on waiting list'- we became trainee mechanics. At least that's what we boasted to those who asked why two boys with a treasured qualification were stuck in the village instead of trying for a 'government job' and, with it, 'security'.

Not that many did ask: the villagers had struggles of their own and we were two ordinary boys who occasionally lazed about but didn't cause trouble. Stinking Tree was like many others in St Vincent and the Grenadines then. It was small, tight, happy, but poor. There was a timeless air about it, things moved at the speed of gossip, not of light.

In our community, even Mrs Mack was well-off. A small, stout, yellow-Carib woman, she grew bananas, yams, avocadoes and oranges for the main market in the capital, Kingstown. Mr Sutton, a permanently-happy widower, raised cows, pigs, chickens and goats for the Saturday market in nearby Georgetown where you had to be up at dawn or you risked returning home empty-handed or with a bowlful of gristle and bones.

Apart from these two and the shopkeepers, Mr Haywood and Mrs Snagg, of whom we were openly proud, everyone else scratched a living. My family grew tannias, corn and dasheen on the tiny plot beside our wooden house and traded with a neighbour for onions, mint, sweet potatoes or green peas. Others did the same, surviving mainly on a diet of vegetables and fruit.

Fish and meat were the problem. Most households raised a handful of scrawny chickens that stepped on your feet in the haste to get at their daily diet of rice grains and morsels of soaked bread. But there were too many Sundays in the year for the chickens to last.

Entertainment was basic and homemade. If you were lucky, a neighbour might let you listen to her radio. Or, from a distance from the porch and through the net curtain, Augustus Campbell charged ten cents to watch the flickering horizontal lines on his black-and-white television. But for the television and radio, village life went on the way I imagined it had done for decades.

Ordinary boys who didn't have enough money to venture often outside the village, Ralph and I were caught in the phase where we were beyond boys, but had no wish to be men. Whenever Mr Roban's decrepit Land Rover refused to start or developed another oil leak, he would send for us and, grateful for the opportunity to get our hands dirty, we would be mechanics for a day. We considered ourselves proper men at such times, men with real jobs, not like the vagabonds who only gave their labour when their money ran out, or who saw nothing wrong in claiming a ram that had strayed into their yard, or stealing a chicken for a cook at the beach.

On one of the rare days when the Land Rover worked without incident, we spent our time with Mr Belto in Georgetown, fetching spanners, positioning the jack, or tightening the huge wheel nuts on his truck. When he was busy with 'paperwork' he would let us change the oil or fan belt or tune the engine. Best of all, when he was in a good mood, he would throw us the keys and I would drive the ten miles to Owia with Ralph driving back to the applause of those who recognised us.

Hands smeared with oil and grease, a day with Mr Belto taxed every muscle in the body. The highlight of the week, working on trucks was where we saw our future. Lacking their size and complexity, cars and vans couldn't compete; they were for *ordinary* mechanics. Our daily tasks completed, we would trudge up the hill from the main road to Stinking Tree, drawing attention to our weariness, nodding at anyone who acknowledged our day's labour. Real mechanics, at least in our eyes, we would bathe for an hour at the public pipe, removing oil and grease with slow care, before joining the boys of our age on the 'branka' at Mrs Seaton's to see the evening through.

Ralph's father owned two acres of land in Lot 14, ten miles

from the village where the mountains began, and he often berated us for pretending we were mechanics when we could be training to become farmers. For agriculture was the future, why hadn't they taught us that at school? They argued often, privately and in public, Ralph trembling to control himself, the old man staring at his son with a mixture of pity and contempt.

'Is only two acres of stupid land,' Ralph would scoff at his father's suggestion of its potential, 'now if was ten acres, you would have something to talk about.'

I took care not to agree with Ralph in front of his father for it was two acres more than my family had. No matter that part of it was hilly and inaccessible, with coconut trees that appeared to reach the sky, land was land, and I would have swapped places with him anytime.

Once, the lanky coconut trees had the space all to themselves; but from the fifties they have been obliged to share the hilly terrain with bananas. Thousands upon thousands of bananas, 'green gold', bound for Barbados and cold Europe. The tall and the short, bananas within reach, coconut trees that even the bravest boys wouldn't climb for a crisp dollar, the contrast is striking.

'Blasted bananas,' Ralph used to swear, 'eat them green, eat them ripe, they taste just the same. I'm a coconut man, give me a refreshing coconut any day.'

Naturally, he couldn't climb those on his father's plot: only the little boys who didn't understand danger would attempt the journey, bear-hugging the corrugated trunks and forcing their way into the heart where the coconuts bunched. The boys looked like enormous frogs to begin with, then, with distance, gradually shrunk until they seemed to have been plucked by the sky.

'Fool,' Ralph once declared, as we watched a boy rush a tree for a meagre dollar, 'why waste time on a giant when you could get to know a *lady*?'

A species of coconut that matured to just over six feet, Spanish coconuts were, naturally, popular in every district. Yellow and smooth, the coconuts could be plucked by anyone but a child. Dwarf coconuts, everyone else called them, but to Ralph they were 'ladies', Spanish ladies. 'The Spanish lady is the sweetest,' he would declare after drinking two or three, 'you can keep your tall breed.' I didn't share his enthusiasm but that didn't bother him: we were friends and one day, he promised, he would convert me to the joys of these special ladies. How were we to know that they would lead him along a dark and lonely road?

With a common coconut Ralph had a 'three- chop' technique: the first a near-vertical motion of the slim machete sharpened 'back and belly' to remove the thick outer husk, the second, a slice rather than a chop, to carve a hole through the inner shell. The third, with the tip of the machete, would forge an opening to the nectar inside the white spherical shell. On a bad day it might require a further twist of the machete's pointed blade to widen the circular hole, but never the seven, eight, nine or even ten clanging blows it took me before I could drink. But with the Spanish ladies he was different, delicate, patient: chopping was too vulgar for them, you had to treat them gently.

With the machete held horizontally, he would make a vertical incision in the head of the heart-shaped coconut with gentle twists of the belly of the machete, then prise apart the tightly-matted husk. Placing the shiny blade carefully on the ground beside him, he would strip the bitter outer husk with his teeth and hands to reveal, in time, the perfectly formed spherical kernel. The shell exposed, he would then proceed to peel away with his penknife any slight deformities.

Shaving the shell was next, a slow job with him, for fear of a rupture. Like a trained surgeon, after fifteen minutes or so, he would pause, consider, then pierce a tiny hole in the top of the soft skull with the penknife. The final incision made, he would tilt his head backwards and begin to drink.

Watching this ritual, fascinated by the elaborate preparation, by his patience, by his air of reverence, part of me wished he would hurry up, the other that he would take his time and prolong the ritual. When he had had enough he would pass the coconut to me and begin with another. I would drink the remainder as he wiped the blade clean. At his signal I would begin to hack away at my share of coconuts in my impatient way.

'Spanish lady,' I would say, wiping away the water flowing down my chin, 'coconut is coconut!'

One Thursday morning in February of the following year, Ralph and I were in Mrs Snagg's shop. The shop stocked everything we needed in the village. Stacked roughly under the counter were sacks of cement and, on shelves one and two, rum and black wine. The smell, simultaneously enticing and off-putting, reached us as we stood by the door. It was ten o'clock and a morning drizzle had sent those nearby scurrying for shelter in the shop. We had been promised a day's work on the Land Rover but, because of the rain, Mr Roban had decided to wait for the weekend.

Another Thursday to see off, and probably a soul-destroying Friday as well, I thought to myself, wishing I had made more of an effort to get into secondary school. I glanced at Ralph and saw that the rain had affected his mood also, souring a promising day. As he took off his proud blue mechanic's overall, I could hear him muttering to himself. The lightest shower and everything came to a standstill, he grumbled, village people had to grow out of this habit: it was childish, we were like people afraid of the dark.

As the rain eased he was still grisly. I had heard rumours that his father had been pleading with him again to help out on the land. It was fertile land, Mr Emmanuel had said in exasperation, the future belonged to agriculture; weeding, ploughing and digging were 'old time', the hoe had been consigned to the shed.

But Ralph wanted something more alluring, something he could do for himself. He wanted to be his own man, to try something, to earn his living by his own hands. The day he got up and didn't get excited about the feel of cold metal in his hand, he promised his father, he would burn his overall and, before the sun was up, he would join him on the land.

Until that time he was going to be a mechanic, stripping down engines and then re-assembling them, watching the black hearts stutter to life, feeling proud that we had mastered what was written in the foreign vehicle manuals Mr Belto hid from us. He had to try; there was no shame in failure, only in not having a go.

That Thursday morning Ralph was more agitated than I had ever seen him. Another day watching the rain, listening to Jim Reeves on the radio or talking about engines we might never get an opportunity to tackle, was too much for him to take.

'How about a trip to see some ladies?' he asked, quietly, so that others couldn't share our secret, 'they must be missing us.'

That suggestion seemed to cheer him up but the thought of slippery grass and a muddy field didn't appeal to me.

'Tomorrow,' I replied, 'you can't really appreciate ladies when it's wet like this.'

I hated the rain and the dark clouds suggested rain for a month.

'Come on,' he said, grabbing me roughly by the arm, 'I can't take another day in this forsaken place.'

I went reluctantly, not knowing that it was to be our final day together. For three miles we walked in near-silence through the persistent drizzle. But by the time we got to the coconut field we had both cheered up. The large, green banana leaves offered some shelter and it wasn't long before we were drinking coconut water, the sweet nectar running down our chests.

'See,' Ralph grinned, 'told you would be worth it.'

I had to agree with him. The trees were nice and short, the coconut water cold and flavoursome. I had wrenched the yellow coconuts from a bunch and laid them out at the foot of the tree. Three each, for we never picked more than we needed. After drinking two, Ralph stood up and stretched noisily as though his body had stiffened up from squatting to prepare the coconuts.

'What about crossing the river and trying out the ladies over there?' he suggested, 'I hear they even sweeter – if that is possible!'

He smiled and slapped me on the back, and I got his meaning.

But I had heard rumours that the owner had a cruel streak, that he had chased two sisters, eleven and thirteen, who had taken a short cut to the river through his land, brandishing a cutlass and threatening to relieve them of their girlhood. A week later, he had slaughtered two cows and a pregnant sow that had 'trespassed' on his land, sent for the owners, and dumped the carcasses in the river in their presence.

'That man too wicked,' I said to Ralph, 'Evil is his middle name. Let's go home.'

He was aware of the man's reputation too but that didn't bother him, he said. Besides, who in their right mind was going to leave their home on a rainy day to check their bananas or coconuts? Would Arthur James do it? Didn't we leave Sam Prince sheltering in the shop? Was Cecily De Santos going to bother about her bananas in this weather when she could be in the comfort of her home sipping a small rum? I saw his point, but my mind was made up.

Determined to go, Ralph shook the coconut debris from his clothes.

'Come on,' he begged, 'come on nuh! Just this time.'

I didn't want to. My clothes were soaked, I was full, and all I desired was to change into something dry.

'What you going home to do,' he asked without bitterness, 'sleep?'

He knew me well, was aware of the effect rain had on me, how much it made me long for the wooden sofa next to the open window in the little 'board house' I shared with my parents, two sisters and three brothers.

'Let's go home,' I tried to persuade him, 'we'll go and see the ladies across the river another time. And we'll spend the whole morning, not just a couple hours. If the sun come out we'll go tomorrow.'

But he wasn't listening. His eyes had the look of someone who was not to be dissuaded.

'Tell you what,' he said, grabbing his machete and cleaning the blade by slicing it through a discarded coconut shell, 'I'll drop a couple off for you later. What you say to that?'

I smiled and said, 'Nah, don't bother. They taste better just from the tree.'

'Your loss.'

Machete in his right hand, he stepped gingerly onto the first stone, stretched out his right foot for the second and, in less than a minute, he was on the other side of the tiny river. I watched him climb the wire fence, machete aloft, his long thin body displaying remarkable skill and balance. A triumphant wave of the machete as he landed on the other side of the fence, then he disappeared. I waited for a minute or so then hurried home.

We are born, we are bound to die.
We are born, we are bound to die.
We are born, we are bound to die.

The 'mourners' were singing and humming this over and over when, at seven that evening, I entered the room where Ralph's body was laid out on a bed that seemed too short for him. In the stifling room, candles flickering, there was a stench of candle wax, camphor, perfume and sweat. Ralph looked ash-grey, as though all the blood had been drained from his young black frame. A white oval bandage ran from the middle of his head to the bottom of his chin as though his jaws needed to be supported. I don't know why, but I expected him to open his eyes to acknowledge my arrival. I was his best friend, surely he would recognise his best friend.

I stood by the bed feeling guilty, foolish and ashamed.

'Sorry Ralph,' I felt like saying, 'sorry.'

I wanted to flee the room. If there wasn't such a crowd I would have run until I was miles away. But I felt trapped, by the people on chairs or on the floor and by my feelings of complicity. I stood there motionless, unable to look directly at my friend.

A few hours earlier we had been together, but I had abandoned him and now he was alone forever. Ralph Emmanuel, trainee mechanic, seventeen, gone.

The woman who had found him in the field had fainted at the sight of the wound to his chest, I heard a man whisper below the humming. He had seen many things in his seventy-nine years but he too would have passed out from the description he had heard of the wound. 'It was an act of the utmost cruelty,' he said, 'it was wicked, evil, it was the work of a disciple of Satan.'

Seeing Ralph in the bed, dressed in white pyjamas for the public, I was glad I had resisted going to the field to see him for the ordeal had obliterated all expression from his face. No pain, no anguish or surprise, no time for a final plea to his maker. Such an empty face, where had the boy who loved engines fled?

I felt guilty, for I knew that, had I really tried, I could have saved him. I stared at him for another minute then I had to leave. I couldn't stay long in the room with all those people and my dreadful secret. I could have saved him, could have snatched his machete and run off with it. A stronger runner, by the time he caught me, we would have been back in the village.

'I could have saved him, I could have saved him,' I kept repeating to myself, as I prepared to sidle away, 'I could have grabbed his arm and dragged him back to the village.'

He might have resisted for a while, might even have pushed me away, but he would have returned with me. From the top of the hill at New Adelphi we might have spent the afternoon watching the sea and dreaming of distant lands. And there were always engines to talk about if nothing else took our fancy. I could have saved him, should have seen Death marching along the road and directed him to another village.

When I eventually left, a woman from Meek Village followed me outside. After the stuffiness and sweat of the room it was a relief to breathe the pure, warm night air. For about two minutes we stood there, together, in the unpitched road staring at the acres of bananas and coconuts in the valley below and at the faint lights of Park Hill in the distance.

'For a few coconuts?' she asked, as though she needed someone to talk to, 'you would kill a young boy for a few coconuts? You would slash a seventeen-year old boy, carve him up like a wild animal, leave him there bleeding in the rain then go home and eat your dinner like nothing happen? A preacher man at that! A man charged with saving souls, yet he could destroy a young life and go home and play with his children!'

I could see she wasn't expecting an answer so I let her continue.

She turned to me and I met her gaze. Ralph had fallen onto his machete and bled to death, she said, that had been the preacher's story; he had died by his own hand. Could anyone believe that? He, the preacher, had gone to check his bananas and had come across a figure huddled over a dozen coconuts. His arrival had startled Ralph. As the young man tried to flee, he had slipped and fallen onto his own machete.

But she knew *he* had killed Ralph, she said through gritted teeth, she knew the preacher from Diamond was guilty and she wanted me to let the whole world know.

On the Sunday, a 'delegation' from the village went to see Mr Emmanuel at six in the morning. They *demanded* 'satisfaction' for Ralph. Alfred Burke was there, Tie Up, Lattie Herbert and Maud Pemberton, two 'Mothers' in the village church, and Yellow Corner and Gustus Cozier who would do anything for their village.

A huge man, quiet, strong, teetotal, usually slow to rouse, Tie Up didn't need encouragement that morning. He lived at the 'top' of the village with his five dogs and was seen only on his way to and from work.

'Just tell me what you want,' he said to Mr Emmanuel, 'just tell me what you want me to do to the preacher. I will go to Diamond and fix him there or bring him right here to you. I can have him here in three hours.'

'Thanks, Tie Up, but leave him,' Ralph's father replied, 'leave him to me. I will fix him. I will fix him good and proper.'

first, second, first, third

'I'm going to form a band, you know,' Sister announced to her
youngest sister one Sunday morning at breakfast, as though the
idea had just come to her, although she had been thinking about
it for a month, 'what you think, Sis?'

'You, Sister, form a band? How you going to do that?'

'Simple: I'm going to have a audition and find the best four-
five musician. '

'In Fitz-Hughes?'

'Right here in Fitz-Hughes.'

'Girl, you must be crazy.'

'No, I'm serious.'

'Cast your mind back ten years: you remember the Providence
Brothers? You remember how they buy drum and organ and
guitar?'

'Yes.'

'And what happen?'

'The band last a month, the brothers square up to fight in the middle of the road, it take three men to separate them.'

'Exactly. You wasting your time, Sister, this is Fitz-Hughes.'

'That was then, Sis, time and season change.'

'Fitz-Hughes people don't.'

'Don't be so negative, the village have talent.'

'Yes, but could they use it?'

'Well, I'm going to show them the way. My band going to put Fitz-Hughes on the SVG map.'

'Who going to do the singing?'

'I'm going to do that.'

'You, Sister, you?'

'Yes me. Me self.'

'But you can't sing.'

'I used to sing in church, didn't I?'

'Yes, with a whole choir to drown out all your false notes and mistakes.'

'Well is the same principle: I can't sing but I can hold a tune. To besides, a good band can always carry a singer.'

'Lord help Fitz-Hughes.'

Blame Alford Dean, he was the one who gave Sister the idea. Not directly, but he was the inspiration behind her plans.

Alford grew up in Trinidad. Farmer, builder and carpenter, in the days when carpenters made solid chairs and tables and built coffins for the dead of the village, Alford was a genuine all rounder. He prospered in all trades. Eligible and skilful, his years in 'South', Trinidad, lent him a sense of mystery; he charmed men and women alike.

Forty-four years and single, Sister wasn't interested in him as a man. He was too thin for her taste, too vulnerable in a gust of wind. She could forgive his smoking and the light-brown moustache he was forever shaping, like a man on the way to a hot dance: after all, a man has to have an interest. But his drinking? No! No! No! She couldn't take that. He drank so much on Saturday nights that every Sunday morning he would apologise to each adult he met on his daily journey through the village in case he had insulted them the previous night.

Sobering up in his front yard one Sunday morning, Sister had witnessed him playing the guitar, a cigarette between the lips, his breakfast of scrambled eggs and fried plantains half-finished on the floor by his chair, and been captivated by the delicacy and crispness of the notes. The contrast between the haggard Alford, shoeless, shirt torn, trousers unbuckled, and the clarity of the music had bewitched her. He was a natural, it was clear, a man with his gift had to be a good teacher. Fitz-Hughes would have a band, she had decided there and then, Alford would be the tutor and she would lead it.

Fitz-Hughes hadn't always been quiet. In the sixties it boasted one of the fiercest 'monkey men' on the leeward coast, Garfield Snagg. To this day people still talk of the 'battles' between Pang Yenny of Troumaca and Garfield. His skin blacked up beyond recognition with charcoal, chained around the waist, and with a red pepper clenched in the teeth, it required two of the village's strongest men to restrain Garfield during Carnival. Children were too frightened to leave their homes on the days he was performing; some of the adults he worked with approached him then as you would a cobra in your path.

Pure theatre, the Garfield of the festivities was magnificent, beautiful and magical. Terrified of the dancing, screaming man reviving an African tradition he didn't fully understand, even his children struggled to recognise their father when he took on this persona.

When the two men clashed in a neutral village, as they did in Coles Hill in 1968, the fight was so intense, so fierce and dramatic, that those present talked about it for a year. That contest ended in a draw, the two men, exhausted, almost dead on their feet, dancing and embracing at the finish like two ancient warriors.

Expectation soared to unprecedented heights. The 1969 encounter, another spectacular, was also drawn. Without collusion neither man appeared again until the mid-seventies, older, weaker, but still with enough fire and spirit to keep the children locked up at home. Fitz-Hughes had been quiet for too long, Sister warned Sis, it was time it made a noise. A local band was years overdue.

Scheduled for ten on the second Sunday in January, the audition to find a band began just under an hour late. Not bad for people with so little respect for time, Sister told herself as she took her seat, if things went well they'd be away by two o'clock. She had rented the community centre and, with the promise of food and drink, the hall was packed, the curious easily outnumbering the performers. There were children and adults from all corners of the village and, inevitably, a smattering from Chateaubelair and Cedars who, having seen the flyer advertising the event, had come to feed and heckle.

With Alford on her right at a desk on the stage that Sunday, they looked a formidable pair of judges, Sister wasn't too modest to admit. New notebooks neatly lined and a spare pen in their breast pocket, she couldn't help feeling important. The postmistress was about to make a name not only for herself but also for the tiny 'village under the volcano'.

She was under no illusion. Talent alone is never enough; without hard work and commitment you might just as well not begin. She had given herself the job of spotting and guiding those with ability. Tutored by Alford and with her backing, the band would be the envy of Chateaubelair, she told herself, as they waited for the audition to begin, the chatterers of Belmont, Prospect and Mangrove would have some excitement in their dull lives. Within a year, Sister began to dream, her group would be playing at weddings, parties and hotel events. If their luck held, they might even conquer the Grenadines!

Mr Rat was the first to perform. An inch shy of five feet, and with a tiny oval head and large ears, he was disqualified on at least two counts Sister could think of as he mounted the stage. He was from Enhams for a start, not Fitz-Hughes, and he already had his own band. Instantly recognisable by his size, he travelled the coastal roads of St Vincent and took the ferry to Bequia and Union Island with his banjo, without ever having to put his hand in his pocket for the fare. The merest mention of an event and he'd be there offering his services.

How many Christmases had Sister been awoken by the sweet strumming of his banjo? How many times had Mr Rat cursed her father for the miserly dollar he had put into the hat after he had serenaded the house for ten minutes? A born musician, he sang and played as he took his meals, he serenaded from village to village. Like a man with a mission to entertain, he even strummed the banjo on the bus. He wouldn't be in the band, everyone knew, but she let him play: he would set the scene nicely, the hopefuls would appreciate the standard to which they had to aspire.

Like the accomplished performer he was Mr Rat strummed and sang with an easy control of voice and music. One moment he was caressing the strings, the next plucking them with such rhythmic force Sister feared they might snap. She watched him dance about the stage, light on his feet, with the vitality of a twenty-year old. In a ten-minute medley he paid tribute to his wife for their nine beautiful children, he cursed the state of the roads in Park Hill and Gorse, he warned of the dangers of rum and beer.

What a start to the show, Sister said to herself proudly as he finished his second song, let them follow that! Rapturous applause and requests for songs from his repertoire were expected and they duly came.

'Thank you, thank you,' he said, acknowledging the audience's generous appreciation, 'but I'm going to give you all an exclusive for my last number. This is a number I've been working on for a year. I hope you like it. It call *I Big For My Size*.'

Sister was familiar with his work. A song could be innocent-sounding but underneath lurked a word or phrase deliberately inserted to 'spice' things up. Anticipating such a song from the title, Sister held up a regal hand and the introductory plucking froze.

'Two cold beers for Mr Rat,' she commanded her son.

A strapping seventeen-year old in a red string vest, Brother rose from his seat in the front row, marched to a large aluminium drum by the stage, and began to delve noisily. With a broad smile that said, 'Come on, you know I deserve more than that,' Mr Rat held up three fingers to Sister. She acknowledged his request and swiftly transferred the gesture to Brother. Her son dug deeper into the drum until he came up with another beer. As Brother carried the three beers to Mr Rat Sister started a second wave of applause. Mr Rat doffed his felt hat, strummed the banjo triumphantly in a grand finale, and withdrew to the cool air outside.

Harvey John was next with his 'baha', five feet of hollow cylindrical wood. A tall man with a pointed head and a toothy grin, he had dressed for the occasion in his best church clothes - white shirt, green trousers, and brown size-15 shoes. Sister didn't care for the long ordinariness of the baha and as for Mr John, the village baker, she could only sigh at his gall: which band was he going to join with that long wooden homemade instrument? A large intake of breath to fill his enormous lungs and before Sister could give the signal he was off, forcing shallow tuneless notes from the baha.

'Booor, booooor, boor,' he went, 'boooor, boorrr, boor.'

Baker or baker-not, two minutes of his puffing was all Sister could take.

'Booor, booooor, boor, boooor, boorrr, boor.'

Motioning to the bucket, she directed Brother to select a soft drink. Like a man who had aimed low and missed even then, or who considered his talent wasted on philistines, Mr John snatched the cold bottle, placed the baha over his right shoulder and stormed off without looking back. No applause, but, thankfully, Sister thought as she crossed him off the list, no booing, or shouts for him to stick to baking bread and cakes for a living, or to put the baha to good use in a fire for Monday's loaves.

Grantley James followed, then Elman Huggins, the first with a harmonica, the other with an ancient, twisted saxophone on which he struggled to lay a finger. With a sympathetic smile Brother offered them two soft drinks of their choice for their pains. Rita Clarke with her drum kit, Claris Major with a battered tenor pan: a cold beer each. It got steadily worse. Vernon Mills fled the stage when he couldn't remember the song he was due to sing, Eldon Billingy abandoned his midway when he realised that he had pitched the chorus way above his capabilities.

What did I do to deserve this? Sister began to fret, which man, woman or beast did I kill? A hard-earned ten dollars to rent the community centre, a small fortune for beer and soft drinks, big-big Sunday, sensible people listening to the radio, relaxing in their garden, or preparing for an afternoon at the beach, and where was she? Imprisoned in a sweltering room listening to the most shameless, untalented bunch of pretenders it had ever been her misfortune to see and hear. An hour and a half and not even a half- good musician! If Fitz-Hughes had talent, where the hell was it hiding?

'I'm getting a headache,' she said to Alford who was sitting back in his chair, a picture of calm, arms folded about the chest as though he had nothing else to do all day, 'these people couldn't play ring-play in moonlight. Let us call off the show.'

'Relax, Sister, it still have people waiting to perform.'

'What people?' she consulted her list. 'Liz Lincoln with a

tambourine she probably steal from the church in Ratho Mill, Noel Greaves with a piano that need to see a dentist, and Bertram Warren who compose a dozen love songs every single day? You have time to waste or what?'

'You have to be patient, Sister.'

'Patient? Is good money it take to put on this showcase in case you didn't notice. Two hundred dollars of my savings from that wretched post office. And for what, this puppet show?'

'Patience, Sister. At least give Bertram a chance.'

'Why?'

'He have potential.'

'This is a audition, not a confessional. You want him to drive everybody home early for their Sunday lunch?'

'Let him play Sister, give him a chance. Don't forget he record a song at *Black Point Studios* two years ago.'

Bertram Warren was a watchman on the Gonsalves estate. He had spent three hundred dollars making a record. The complimentary copies were popular with his relatives and friends but the bulk remained in a suitcase under his wooden bed.

'All right,' Sister agreed, 'but the moment he start to crow about his family, he off.'

Sister nodded to indicate to him that he was next and Bertram approached the stage with a confidence not seen since Mr Rat.

It didn't take long to come round to Alford's point of view. Bertram's song was basic, but even to her inexperienced ear, it had something, an undefined simplicity that didn't tax the listener. Easy to sing along to, it would be just as easy to dance to. First chord, higher, first chord again, lower. Four minutes of Bertram's simple lament for the wife driven away by his gambling and drinking, the last verse proclaiming a religious conversion and his desire to win her back, had the audience almost as spellbound as it had been by Mr Rat.

Sister was impressed. She relaxed in her chair and tapped her feet to the chorus. The music was elementary, catchy, quick to latch on to. 'Sweet' was the word everyone used to describe Mr Rat's music, vitality driving every chord. Bertram's song was uncompromisingly sentimental, yet it was inspired, the work of a man crying out to be listened to. 'I coming back,' he sang, a threat to his wife, or a promise, Sister couldn't decide which, 'I coming again.' Whatever he meant it sounded good: it would be one of their standards.

Sister shook Alford's hand then placed a huge exaggerated tick against Bertram's name: finally they were on the way.

'First,' Sister nodded approvingly as Bertram threaded his way through a final, extemporised, verse extolling the virtues of married life, 'first, second, first, third.' She strummed an imaginary guitar under the table, moving her fingers along the fret and hearing the music in her head. 'First, second, first, third.'

The beginnings of a band began to take shape in her mind. Hope at last. Two more musicians of Bertram's calibre and they were made.

'Three beers for Bertram,' she gestured to Brother, 'and a soft drink as well!'

To spontaneous applause, Bertram left the hall clutching his reward and his guitar.

Within a week practice had begun. Warner Ellis, a seventeen year old Methodist was recruited to play the drums and Morgan Riley, a police cadet who had somehow found his way in, the steel drums and percussion. Bertram played the guitar and shared the writing and singing with Sister, and Osric Green, a customs officer, the saxophone.

Weeks into the rehearsal Sister allowed herself to dream. 'A, B, A, C: First, second, first, third,' she would drive the band on, her increasingly confident voice plugging the gaps in the music, her suggestive dancing forcing another verse from their tired fingers or voices, 'we have it, we doing it, I feel it. Don't stop now!'

Fuelled by rum, beer and mauby one night, they made such a beautiful noise that she became light-headed with joy. The dream had moved on, the band had become real. Another warm evening she had almost fainted with pleasure at the harmony they had managed to sustain throughout the ten minutes of the song. They had arrived, there was no going back.

They practised on Tuesdays and Fridays, sometimes for two hours and, if the mood dictated, three. Five songs made up their repertoire. Sister had seen bands blighted by overambition, counting bookings and money before they were competent, boasting of venues they were going to play. *Sister and the Brothers* wouldn't be like that; new to the rigours of public entertainment, they respected their limitations. Forty minutes up and down the scales with five numbers, it was better not to overreach themselves. They would play what they knew, and play it well. If an audience wanted more, they would perform the songs in a different order, varying the tempo, or lengthening a passage with improvised patches of singing and dancing.

Onlookers and supporters were amazed. Originally sceptical, in the early weeks, they had hung around the community centre waiting for false starts, arguments and for the folding of the band. They vied to be present when the bust-up came, saw each session as potentially the last.

They waited patiently on Tuesdays, were back after work on Friday. They waited in vain. What they were witnessing was new to Fitz-Hughes. Sceptics became supporters. For determination if nothing else, the band deserved a chance. Seven months later, *Sister and the Brothers* was ready to go public.

Samuel Richardson lived in Canada. Fifty-three, arthritic, freshly-divorced, he had returned to St Vincent and the Grenadines for a short break instead of his annual summer camping trip to Montreal. Holidaying in the Caribbean for the first time in twenty-six years, he was too experienced a man to travel alone in his homeland, he said to himself on landing, he needed a guide. His accent was still intact but he had forgotten much. Places and names had been erased from his memory, new buildings had sprung up, vehicles had multiplied. He didn't fancy being caught out and made to look like a simpleton who had never visited the capital.

Then there were the long warm evenings and nights to contend with. Warm Caribbean nights call for conversation; they drag with brandy and beer for company, but flow by with chatter and play. Fools might travel alone but, after a protracted divorce, how could anyone call him a fool?

On the short drive out of the airport building he met Sylvia Temple. Sylvia was the car park attendant at Arnos Vale that day. Extremely good-looking, playful, with a grin that came readily, neat white teeth bared to greet or say goodbye, she had given

Samuel one of her smiles and scribbled her phone number on the back of the car park ticket. Within a week Samuel was promising to return to St Vincent and the Grenadines for good. The arthritis had eased, the shuffle from the crippling pain in his legs also. Without too much effort he could chase down an athletic Sylvia on the beach at Villa, Palm Island and Union Island. Up the stairs to bed was a doddle for the man his ex-wife had publicly labelled 'Saturday Soldier'.

A young-looking twenty-nine, the gap between their ages provoked the occasional second glance and quiet whisper. But Samuel didn't care: in his eyes she was mature, she loved the same games and, her aunt apart, what others said was their concern.

For their private entertainment, what began as a bet to pass the time as they waited one Monday for a guide at the Botanical Gardens, became a part of their daily routine. Sylvia bet Samuel that he couldn't manage a three-course meal at the Bamboo Restaurant, he responded that she'd be tipsy by the time she got to her dessert. She bet that she could beat him at cards, he retaliated that he could swim further out to sea. They bet on the first to spot a plane, and on the price of mangoes at the roadside in Belvedere. Each bet came with a kiss for the winner: Samuel had kisses from his toes to his ears.

Canadian stress swiftly ejected from his shoulders, the sunshine did the rest, thawing out the twenty-six long Toronto winters. He was young again, rejuvenated.

His age matched her stamina. Old enough to be her father, yet he was her lover! Younger men could only look on with envy, holding out their hands to touch hers as she passed them, only to end up with empty palms. Her birthday was approaching; Samuel had found the perfect present for the woman with the cheeky grin.

He had hired a hall at Belvedere, small, but spacious enough for the ninety invited guests, some old school friends, others newly acquired, her family and friends. Dressed as though for a wedding, there to witness the public yet discreet declaration of his feelings for Sylvia, the guests mingled freely. Strangers were soon friends. As they took their places for dinner Samuel smiled lovingly at Sylvia who was sitting with an aunt a discreet distance away, and she responded with a beam from ear to ear. Such joy, such heaven! She was his beloved: if only her aunt knew the full story!

He had certainly made an impression with her uncle Neil. The uncle had made a point of shaking his hand, inviting him for a drink in Owia later that week and 'threatening' to introduce him to the rest of the family. Sweet heaven!

Those poor people in Toronto suffering in the cold, Samuel thought to himself as he stood at the entrance to the hall after the meal, clutching a beer and grinning with the self-importance of a first-time returner, he was going to sell up, build a house in Fitz-Hughes and settle down with Sylvia. Her knee-length orange birthday dress revealing the curves he had come to appreciate, Samuel relived the evening they had registered as husband-and-wife at the New Montrose Hotel, and the Thursday they had made love at her uncle's house in Fancy while he was fishing off the coast of St Lucia.

Sylvia Temple. Nothing was too good for her. Young, vigorous, beautiful, she deserved the best. A live band to celebrate her birthday was the least he could do after she had cooked him rice and peas for Sunday lunch, made beef roti twice in one week and bakes and scrambled eggs for breakfast every morning. Who had told her that bakes were his favourites? That didn't matter. He indulged her and, in return, she was generous with her time and love. A band from his own village could only add an extra dimension to the occasion.

Sister and the Brothers took to the stage just after seven. Sister was dressed in a yellow trouser suit to show off her ample curves, the 'Brothers' in matching blue, a slight flaring of the trousers recalling the seventies. Their first booking, one hundred dollars paid in advance, a birthday party for 'Samuel's girl'. Sister couldn't help feeling apprehensive. Despite a hearty dinner she still felt empty, hollow, the way she sometimes felt on entering a doctor's surgery, however trivial the complaint. 'Keep calm,' Alford had warned her during the meal, 'stay calm, breathe, breathe. And sing from your bottom-belly, not with your mouth.'

The moment had arrived. Her gaze went to Alford as the guests waited in anticipation. 'Breathe, breathe, breathe.' Alfred counted slowly to four on his left hand and, like a truck with the chock to stop it rolling down a slight incline removed, the band eased away, opening with Bertram's audition number, *I coming back, I coming again.* She made a discreet sign of the cross and said a silent prayer. 'First, second, first third,' she then whispered to the band from the corner of her mouth, 'let's go.' At Sister's whispered command and with the chocks fully removed, away the band sprinted.

Sister drove them through the first verse and chorus and the band responded. Playing for Fitz-Hughes, for their friends and supporters, they played for their lives. With the discipline they had shown in practice they stuck to their lines, no one sought personal glory. The merest hint of a gap in the music or the threat of drifting, and Sister diverted attention with a suggestive roll of the hips.

There was a certain something to the music, she had to admit when they were fully into their stride, it was repetitive but tuneful. It had a confident sound.

The crowd loved it. Dancing off the effect of the lavish three-course dinner, a fast undemanding rhythm with a catchy tune was just the thing. In the middle of the floor Sister could make out Samuel, shirt unbuttoned, a large grey flannel applied to his forehead at regular intervals like a man under a raging fever. He had picked up the chorus quickly, he was clearly enjoying their playing. 'I coming back,' Sister screeched over the sweet drone of the saxophone, 'I coming again.'

A discreet conductor at the front of the stage Alford let them play for twelve minutes. The instant he detected the crowd tiring he gestured, with an imperceptible nod of the head, for the band to move to the next song. They slowed, one instrument eliminated at a time, the drummer closing with soft notes on the cymbals.

'Never give a paying crowd time to breathe between songs,' Alford had warned during the meal, 'once you stop, *they* stop.'

So before the audience could catch its breath and drift to the bar or to conversations, the drummer had launched them into the second number, a three-way collaboration between Sister, Bertram and Alford, *Who don't get don't want.*

The second song was similar to the first, but quieter, allowing for a slower dance, for couples as well as singles. From the stage Sister observed the change in the crowd, of partners and of position. One thing remained, though, the energy of the dance. A warm feeling of pride filled her, the village postmistress was now a bandleader!

The introductory song out of the way, the initial nervousness under control, the band relaxed and played as they had at rehearsal and practice, with controlled energy and a tight harmony. Holding it together, they looked at each other with quiet satisfaction. 'Who don't get don't want,' they sang, 'who don't get don't want.' During the chorus Samuel began to climb onto the stage. Meeting him halfway, Sister motioned for the band to continue in her absence.

'Could you slow things down a bit?' Samuel whispered in her ear.

'What?' Sister asked, struggling to hear above the music.

'Something slow, can you play something slower?'

'But people dancing, what's the problem?'

'Is not a problem, just that the birthday girl want something more mellow.'

'Mellow like how?'

'Just a bit slower.'

'You didn't say anything about slow music, you just wanted a band to play.'

'But a band must could play everything.'

'This is a dance band,' Sister stood her ground.

'Well play music to dance to then.'

Feeling a bit tetchy Sister returned to the band and conveyed the message. On her command they merged seamlessly into the next song. Admittedly, tune three resembled the second which in turn had differed little from the first. Slower, much slower, and all the more difficult to hold together, she whispered her chant when she felt they were losing momentum or threatening to speed up.

When after two minutes they had settled into a recognisable pattern, like an aeroplane levelling off after a bumpy climb, Samuel gave Sister a nod of approval and went in search of Sylvia. It was her special night, it would be *their* special night.

But he was too late. Sylvia already had partner, a young man of about twenty-five, Samuel guessed. They were dancing slowly, whispering to each other and giggling, as though they had danced many times before. Samuel didn't like it. The idea of his beloved dancing with another man hadn't occurred to him. He prayed that the music would end. She was his, she should be with him, not with some boy in designer jeans and an expensive T-shirt. Four minutes later, the band still going, he could stand it no longer. He went to get another beer.

When he returned she was in relaxed conversation at the entrance to the hall. As Samuel approached, her companion eased away.

'Who was that?' he asked.

'Who?'

'That man.'

'What man?'

'The man you were talking to. The man sitting in that red car over there.'

'Oh, Vincent? He works in the bank in Argyle.'

'What you doing out here with him?'

'Out where?'

'Out here. What so important you have to come outside?'

'This isn't outside, I just came to the door for some fresh air.'

'So why he had to come with you, he's your bodyguard or something?'

'Don't be ridiculous!'

'And who was that you were dancing with earlier?'

'You mean Nibert?'

'The man in the yellow shirt.'

'He's my cousin. He is Aunty Effy's son. She's the tall woman with the glasses who used to live in Holland? '

'Lucky Holland.'

'Don't be like that, she's my favourite aunt. Let's go inside.'

'Sylvia, I'm not stupid, you know, I see how men behave when you are around, I see how they look at you.'

'That is their problem. Men don't bother me.'

'Well they bother *me*!'

'Only if you foolish enough to let them. Look, Samuel, sweetheart, you have nothing to hot up yourself about.'

'You sure that man is your cousin?'

'I ever lie to you?'

'No. And you better don't start now.'

'You have to trust me, sweetheart.'

'I do, Sugar, I do. But I didn't know who they were, that's all.'

Sylvia placed her right hand at the back of his neck, drew him close to her then kissed him on the right cheek.

'Trust me, sweetheart. You have to trust me.'

Samuel took her by the shoulders.

'Come on,' he said, 'I request a special song just for you and me. Should be coming up any time now.'

'What the song call?'

'I don't know the name only that it mellow.'

'Mellow how?'

'Just mellow enough to show you how I feel. Let's go inside and have a dance.'

'I don't know. It wouldn't feel right dancing 'mellow' in front of all these people.'

'Why, what's wrong with that? You don't have a problem when we together alone.'

'That is different.'

'Different how?'

'This is in public: everybody going to be watching. My aunts, my uncle, my cousins, everybody. And you know how some people eyes long. You know how country people love to gossip and construe.'

'Let them!'

'That might be all right for you but I don't like people calling up my name. Is not as if we engaged. If we were engaged it would be different. We could dance fast, we could dance mellow, nobody going to care.'

'Engaged?'

'Yes, engaged. If we were engaged we wouldn't have to dodge and peep. We would be sitting side-by-side at a table instead of me sitting with my aunt. Then tomorrow you could drive me to work, we could have lunch at *Caroline's Restaurant*, and in the evening you could come and pick me up. And at weekends I could cook you callaloo soup or peas soup or rice and peas or whatever you like.'

'Engaged, Sylvia?'

'Yes, why not?'

'But what about your friends? What about the bank man?

What about your cousin and all the men who peal their eye when you pass by? What about that one who stretch out his hand for you at Byera Bay? You let him stroke your fingers before you pull away!'

'Idiots will be idiots.'

'He was just an idiot, was he?'

'Not an idiot, more like a pest.'

'You shouldn't have let him touch you.'

'They're not men, Samuel, they're just boys. That's all they good for, watching and fattening their eye. Stretching out their hand hoping you would do the same. But don't bother with them, sweetheart, none of them in your rank. They can't come close to you.'

'For truth?'

'For truth. I had boyfriends before you, I'm not going to deny that, but no one I really care for. You're the first man I'm serious about.'

'Not even the bank man?'

'*Especially* not the bank man.'

'And your "cousin"?'

'My "cousin" is just my cousin.'

'And no one else?'

'No one serious.'

'Promise?'

'Promise.'

'Swear to God?'

'Swear to God.'

A roll of the drums signalled that *Sister and the Brothers* had come to the end of their set.

'I coming back,' Samuel shouted for an encore as he led Sylvia by the hand back to the hall, 'I coming again.'

'First, second, first, third,' Sister coaxed the band, 'lewwe go!'

Somewhere in the middle of the dancers she could make out Samuel and Sylvia locked at the waist, turning, twisting, her left leg in the air and his right, like a pair of scissors opening and closing rapidly. They made a lovely couple. For skill and inventiveness they were in a class of their own.

A little later, Sister slowed the band. The guests having had their fill of shuffling, sliding and winding for the evening, it was time to get mellow again. For this was not just their night, it was Samuel's also. He had given them their first booking, had paid them handsomely, they had put Fitz-Hughes on the map. He wanted mellow, so mellow it would be.

Eight minutes into the song Samuel and Sylvia were locked together, her arms fastened around his neck like a child clinging to her father for fear of being snatched by a stranger. Sister smiled a quiet, satisfied smile. The band would get at least one more booking before the year was out.

action action

One Saturday afternoon in April 1967, Mrs Goodridge received a letter from her husband in England. Halfway through reading it, a massive headache came on.

'Meena!' she screeched to the young girl who lived with her, 'Meena!'

'Here, Mrs Goodridge.'

'Close up the shop!'

'Yes Mrs Goodridge.'

'Shut the windows in the front room!'

'Yes Mrs Goodridge.'

'And turn off the fire under the pot!'

'What happen, Mrs Goodridge, hurricane coming?'

'Hurricane? What hurricane?'

'You shutting up the shop so must be big storm or hurricane.'

'Don't bother about that girl, just do as you're told.'

'Yes Mrs Goodridge.'

With a low sigh Meena drew in the heavy wooden doors of the shop, bolted the windows, then dragged herself to the kitchen to turn off the gas. Ten minutes later, at two in the afternoon, Mrs Goodridge went to bed.

Mrs Goodridge lived in Dubois. Perched precariously on a hill, away from the main road that still clings to the coast, from the lowest point in the village you can see as far as Bequia to the south and St Lucia to the north.

Rain was their greatest worry. Two years earlier a storm had washed away chickens, cattle and goats and a sandy section of the lower village, depositing them unceremoniously on Pennington Valley below. So, like a tree that might tumble under a single chop at its root or lower body, the people of Dubois always felt one storm away from a landslide.

The British army had a base there in the eighteenth century and, every now and again, while preparing the foundations of a new house, bones would surface. A large sunken skull unearthed in Mr Griffith's back yard one Christmas season had provided speculation and conversation for the month of January. Dubois was like that.

Mrs Goodridge loved her village. Sparsely populated, its three hundred or so inhabitants were wary of strangers. Visitors without the proper name or a convincing description of the person they were seeking were greeted with a shrug of the shoulders and instructed to ask elsewhere.

Two miles of partially concreted track away from the main road, on a steep incline that didn't give, people only went to Dubois to see relatives or on business: fishermen from Layou with fresh sprats or jacks, Mr Warner, the baker from Sandy Bay with warm bread, Mrs Woodley from Calder with medicines for all ailments. On a quiet Saturday few said, 'Let's take a walk up to Dubois, nuh.' If Tuesday dragged no one suggested that, 'There's a netball tournament in Dubois, might be worth a peep.' Where other villages vied to be heard, Dubois slept contentedly. It suited Mrs Goodridge perfectly.

When she woke up on the Sunday the headache had gone. But, as she opened the shop promptly at eight, she felt anxious and jittery. Her husband had been in England for twelve years, why didn't he just stay there?

She was so lucky, she used to boast to her circle of women - Martha Roban, the midwife, Lacy Neverson, the preacher and Millicent Boucher, who sold flowers for weddings and funerals. When they met up monthly at the back of the shop or at another's home, with ginger beer and banana fritters, she was lucky, she would boast, she was probably the most fortunate of them all. Her blood pressure was fine, her appetite was good, she avoided the eddoes and dasheen that clogged up her digestive system. A brisk walk around the village before going to bed hardly got her heart racing.

Sharp enough to spot a child preparing to steal a juicy plumrose from the basket at the entrance to the shop, her eyes had years left in them. The hours behind the counter had sharpened the rapid calculations she could perform at twenty. Business was flourishing, she sewed well into the night when inspired. If she fancied it, she could go shopping in Kingstown, leaving Meena in charge. But best of all for a married woman, her husband lived four thousand miles away! What more could she want? Could Millicent or any of the others better that?

When, in one of his letters, her husband complained about the weather in England, the driving rain, the fog and snow, and that his job as a guard meant constant exposure to the elements on the freezing platforms of Charing Cross and London Bridge, she had replied to him, she told her friends, that she had sold her first dress for nine dollars and had already received a payment of five.

New to the country, he had rented a room in Shepherds Bush, sharing the kitchen and bathroom with an Irish tenant, a temporary arrangement until he could afford a place of his own: she had made a dozen pillowcases, had sold four at a dollar each, and was optimistic about orders for a further dozen. The nights were bitterly cold, loneliness was eating him up, he longed for the sun, the sea, and a warm body next to his: the shop now stocked pencils and pens, geometry sets, erasers and exercise books: school uniforms were next, there was a demand in the neighbourhood.

In her own way she loved him, she admitted to Martha, but her passion, sewing, had taken over her life. Being alone held no terrors for her, not with the shop to look after, sheets and pillowcases to mend, and new styles in clothing to attempt. A wife with a distant husband never has things easy, but as long as she could have the gentle murmur of her sewing machine, she had the worries of a bright five-year old girl.

Her husband had left for England a month after their wedding. A cousin of his sister's boyfriend with contacts on the railways, had promised to put in a word on his behalf. London was calling out for train drivers, he had written, fellows from Barbados and Jamaica went straight from the boat-train at

Waterloo to driving trains there. Provided that he showed the necessary aptitude, there'd be no problem.

Alfred Goodridge had inherited his mother's shop. Plump at thirteen, and growing rounder with each year, as a boy he wasn't physical. A scorer at sports or a vocal spectator, smartly dressed whatever the occasion, he was never going to be a physical man. Alfred Goodridge, train driver, tons of solid cold metal under his direct control, hundreds of passengers marvelling at his skill, his friends in Dubois whispering his name as they played cards, draughts or dominoes: what an accomplishment that would be!

The thrill of buying, selling, bartering and haggling was hypnotic, but a train driver would put him in the same league as Marlon Jeffers. Short, bespectacled, ordinary-looking, bald but for a few strands of grey at the back of his head, a lecturer in English at an American university, Marlon was one of the village's favourite sons. On his annual visit home he flirted outrageously with the women during the day and drank their husbands off their chairs at night. From a distance Alfred envied Marlon; he saw himself several ranks above a shopkeeper. He could do the job, he promised his young wife, he had the skill to be a train driver. An unblemished thirteen years in his second-hand *Ford* was the record he would take with him to England.

Within a year, by his expert calculations, he would have saved enough for his wife to join him. If things didn't go to plan, two years at the most. But he failed the train drivers' theory test. Deflated but undaunted, he retired to his room to prepare for a second attempt.

His West Indian friends consoled him.

'Bad luck Goodridge, try again, lots of educated fellas does fail first time.'

That reassured him for a while, but the geography of London was complex, the laws and regulations an unmanageable mass of detail for someone who simply wanted to climb into a train and drive.

He asked for more time. He wanted to be ready, another failure would crush him. In the interval a friend suggested that he shadow a driver for a day and practise in an old engine at the side of the depot. Alfred Goodridge perked up, he was on his way.

In the cockpit of a defunct train, with its smell of stale-oil, old fumes and grease, he felt comfortable, in his rightful place. He could have been behind the counter in the shop or bartering at the market in Kingstown. He forgot himself, he *was* a driver.

But so many instruments! So much to take in! He flicked one switch, pushed another, turned one knob clockwise, its neighbour anticlockwise. He twisted, fiddled, pulled levers and tested the brakes. Under the weight of his left elbow the glass of the speedometer broke; his tugging dislodged the dead phone from its cradle. 'I'll give you some advice, mate,' said the white-bearded Antiguan driver who had been observing his actions with increasing alarm, 'your place is at the back of a train, keep well away from the front.'

A guard lacked the glamour of a driver; at first Alfred felt like an understudy in a silent film. But the job paid well, was relatively undemanding, and allowed him to be near trains for which he was developing a genuine passion. Driving from the back, as it were, he was still in charge of the train, wasn't he?

The uniform fitted him too. Black or navy-blue, it made him

look serious, professional, a man who commanded respect. A wide leather belt restrained his stomach; when polished, the steel toe-capped boots would have made the fussiest soldier proud. As he stood before the mirror in his tiny bedroom adjusting his tie and flicking minute flecks of dust from his jacket, he wished that his wife and friends could see him. So, immediately after qualifying as a guard, he took three photographs of himself in uniform, one for his album, the second for his wife, and the last for the shop.

A step down in ambition, yet he retained the shopkeeper's light tongue: a woman popping into *Goodridge Stores* for matches invariably left with farine, butter and soap, or some other unintended purchase; a farmer stopping by for a petit of rum after a back-breaking day in the mountains ended up with bread, herring-in-tomato-sauce and a soft drink for breakfast the next day. With his natural curiosity, as the passengers waited or enquired about departure times, Mr Goodridge would prolong the conversation, seizing the opportunity to learn little snippets about England and to tell them, and to remind himself, of his position, and to polish his English.

'Excuse me,' a woman asked one Monday afternoon a month into the job, 'could you possibly tell me the time of the next train to Tunbridge Wells?'

'That would be the 5.07, Madam.'

'And after that?'

'The 5.23.'

'And after that?'

'The 5.41.'

'Thank you.'

'My pleasure, my pleasure indeed. There's quite a good service to Kent during the rush hour. Would you like me to get you a timetable?'

'No, no need, I'm fine.'

'Lovely place, Tunbridge Wells.'

'Thank you. Where are *you* from?'

'St Vincent.'

'Where?'

'St Vincent.'

'You mean Jamaica?'

'No, St Vincent.'

'Where's that?'

'In the West Indies.'

'Oh. Right.'

'My wife and I own a store, you know.'

'That's nice.'

'We sell food, stationery and clothes.'

'That's nice.'

'She'll be joining me soon.'

'I'm glad.'

'What's it like in Tunbridge Wells?'

'It's mist, mist and more mist, but it's a wonderful place: I wouldn't swap it for anywhere, not even the South of France.'

Then, without encouragement, out had come photographs of his wife, the store, and himself in uniform. And, despite her initial reluctance, out had come hers too, husband, three children and poodle, before he would let her catch her train.

'Must go now, mustn't be late. But thanks once again.'

'Thank *you*, Madam.'

No passenger was too dull for a chat, no town too remote to declare an interest.

With a guard's salary, it made sense to postpone the reunion; when the time was right he would write to Leela. They had grown up in relative comfort, his wife wasn't going to live in someone else's home: they were from Dubois and Dubois people had pride.

Working overtime, he saved assiduously and suggested that she prepare to join him. Could he delay a little longer? she replied, there were some things she had to fix. The ticket would be posted the moment she gave the word: would he mind if she finished the batch of towels she had promised the church? Always an order to fill or something to complete. To pass the time Mr Goodridge sought new places to eat. The restaurants in Stoke Newington, Kensington and Notting Hill became his haunts. He grew rounder and rounder.

He had bought a house, he wrote the following year, the bedroom windows let in the cold but the renovation was going well, within months it would be ready: how could she give up the business when demand for school uniforms was so great, and when a woman from Basin Hole Village had ordered a dress for her child's baptism? Each invitation was blocked, each suggestion to prepare, rebuffed. Soaring profits, sewing, and with them her reputation, were too important to cast to the wind, Leela wrote back, when she was ready she would let him know.

The invitations to join him dwindled and eventually stopped. Now, after twelve years, when she had almost forgotten that she had a husband, when she had become accustomed to living on her own and to having the width of the bed to herself, they were going to have to share a house!

With trembling fingers, she read the letter again, the first paragraph only, for she couldn't go further, the stylish calligraphy honed in the shop swimming before her eyes, the thought of an amorous Alfred causing her to shiver. She went back to bed.

But she couldn't sleep. Visions of Alfred filled her mind, from the day he left for England, from their 'walking out' days.

Eight months they had walked out before getting married. Precise in his speech, thirty-one, rotund, known in the district as a big eater, Alfred's physique couldn't mask the main pleasure in his life. An ordinary young woman approaching thirty, Leela Campbell had seen something in him that suggested that he wouldn't be too demanding.

His love of food, of dressing up for an ordinary day selling smoked-herring, rum, tarts, rice, flour and butter, his ability to pass long hours in the half-dark behind the counter on quiet Wednesdays without complaint, suggested a man, a kindred spirit, to match her ambition. His pleasures would keep him away from her, she quickly surmised, and hers, sewing, would keep her occupied.

For all the 'love-stuff' other couples went in for didn't agree with her. Caressing, squeezing, hugging, she hated even the thought and sight of them. They were revolting acts. The touch of warm flesh or sweaty palms, she couldn't abide anyone getting close. Her younger sister, Anna, who washed, dried, greased, and combed her hair was the only person who could touch her without her squirming or withdrawing into herself. On folding away the sewing machine she sometimes wished that she could patent a cylindrical dress, about a metre in diameter, that would oblige people to keep their distance.

After five months of walking out, on a hot Sunday afternoon, it happened. May the dreadful day always be tomorrow, she used to pray, let it be tomorrow, or, better still, the day after that. For although diminished in passion, Alfred Goodridge had his 'admirers', she had heard. *Goodridge Stores* was seldom short of women and not all came with enough money for their purchases, a little bird had whispered to her. Janice Baptiste, short and busty, who came to 'listen to the radio' and Nancy Dabriel, 'Janice's company', were bold and barefaced, but she didn't mind: they kept Alfred away from her and they didn't break the shop, so where was the problem?

One day, though, she feared, one evening or night, he would lose control and try to be a man with her. Tomorrow, please Lord, she prayed, please let it be tomorrow.

Returning from the beach one Sunday, slightly groggy from drink or from hours in the sea, she couldn't tell which, he had stumbled into her bedroom with a look in his eyes that made her shudder.

'Leela,' he had shouted, just as she was preparing for her afternoon nap, ' I'm back.'

'Alfred, what kind of noise you making?'

'Noise?'

'You trying to wake the dead or something?'

'You haven't heard noise yet.'

'Oh my Lord, Alfred, what's got into you?'

'Leave the Lord out of it.'

'Alfred, is it really you?'

'Yes Leela, I think the time has come.'

'Time for what?'

'Leela, I am a man and you are a woman.'

'Oh Lord.'

'And you know that that means.'

'Lord help me.'

'What you waiting for?'

'Alfred, please, today is Sunday. Leave it till tomorrow.'

'Leela, I'm a man, and I can't hold onto it any longer.'

'Not on a Sunday, Alfred, any other day.'

'Sunday, Monday, another day and I will burst.'

'Sunday's the Lord's day, Alfred, you must respect that. You must could wait.'

'No Leela, I can't wait: not another day, not another night!'

Leela wasn't in the mood. She was never in the mood. That kind of thing had never interested her. When Martha or Millicent boasted about their nightly cavorting she listened politely, indifferent, slightly bored. The more graphic the descriptions the more convinced she was of the futility and unnaturalness of the whole business.

Perfecting stitches, cutting out patterns, choosing fabrics and selecting threads of different colours and thicknesses were a more profitable use of her time. And now Alfred wanted her to be like any other woman!

If they had to do it she didn't want it to happen *that* afternoon. Dressed for home and not for worldly affairs, she wished that she had taken Millicent's advice that lovers have to 'stay ready'.

Trust Alfred to present himself on the day when she had decided to try on her very first attempt at underwear!

For after years of experimenting with dresses she had turned, in frustration, to underclothing. Hanging on a rail in the bedroom, her first batch of dresses had a primitive, square, look, even *she* had to admit. If clothes could look sad, *they* did.

With openings for arms, legs and neck, despite her best efforts, they invariably ended up one-dimensional, plain, suitable for a woman of her build with modest behind and solid hips. Millicent had declined a complimentary one, Martha's wardrobe 'didn't have room for pyjamas much less a dress'. All that work, so many hours, and each garment had ended up crumpled and pitiful like its predecessor!

Skirts were next. Almost rectangular in design, they had to be easy, hadn't they? But pleats defeated her, and zips were trickier to get right than she had imagined.

The *Singer* machine humming under the rhythm of her feet, underwear had seemed a promising alternative after the disappointment of the first crop of dresses and the difficulties with zips and pleats. Out of sight, 'invisible', it was virtually impossible to go wrong with underwear, wasn't it? Naturally, she would never achieve the intricate garments favoured by the younger women of the village, but there was a market for women like her, wasn't there?

Unfortunately that Sunday, she was wearing her very first effort, yellow, the left leg stitched an awkward two inches above the right, robbing it of its symmetry. With no hope of selling it, and with her shopkeeper's instinct, it had seemed sensible to make use of it herself.

'Leave it till tomorrow, Alfred, I ain't feeling well.'

He was a patient man but she could see that he had built himself up to it and wouldn't be dissuaded.

Her desirability was never in question, she was what she was, what Alfred or others thought of her sexually didn't bother her. Yet she didn't wish to be remembered like this, in outsize, lopsided, yellow, square drawers so poorly constructed that a drunken man would have sobered up at the sight.

Perhaps she could still deflect him, she said to herself, there were some old off-white 'four-stringed drawers', built from a coarse 212lbs flour-bag, in a suitcase she kept under the bed. Perhaps she could retrieve one, ask casually what he thought, in the hope that he might be put off by the sight of the contraption.

A souvenir from her mother, most village women of their era could afford nothing else. Leela had toyed with the idea of reintroducing them for Martha, Millicent and Polly, but had been put off by her failure with more modern and simpler cuts. Starched to voluminous proportions, the 'four-string' offered respite for the woman whose man was too impatient or unskilled to unravel the cords stitched into the circumference of the waist. But it was risky: she had heard that some men enjoyed the gradual erotic disentanglement of the device and would work themselves into a frenzy at the sight of one. What would she do if the Alfred she had once caught stroking Janice's knee turned out to be one of those with a penchant for the unusual?

That Sunday afternoon, then, Leela had drawn the curtains, raced into the bed and turned the radio on full volume. Eyes squeezed tight, she had sung along, in her mind, to the songs on the radio. She remembered a rocking motion, like a boat plunging from one tumbling swell to another on a tumultuous sea, and a feeling of being flattened by a colossal weight.

Three fried eggs, two small loaves, and a steaming cup of

cocoa for breakfast the next morning told her that their fumbling hadn't been a complete calamity. And now, with his return, he would want to recreate that afternoon, wouldn't he? She wasn't Millicent, Janice or Nancy: she was too old for that kind of thing.

It was lucky that she had Meena living with her, she said to herself, as she sought a way to delay the inevitable. Twelve years was a long time but Alfred would have to respect the young girl in the room adjacent to theirs, wouldn't he?

She had found Meena in Peruvian Vale where she often shopped. The figs from this roadside village were tight and juicy, a favourite in Dubois. The moment word got out that they were on sale there would be a rush for them. Laden with figs, a bunch was deceptively heavy, so Meena's mother had sent the young girl to lend a hand. She had stayed with Mrs Goodridge, returning home at Easter and Christmas.

That was three years ago. Meena had set fire to the mango tree in the yard, had taken the dog for a walk one Sunday and lost it and was, at times, a little too womanish for someone of Mrs Goodridge's nature. But she was a good companion and, with weekly private lessons from Mr Bullock, a retired headteacher, her school work was improving. A help in the shop at weekends, she kept the house tidy, she swept the yard without complaint and her cooking was coming along. Unlike her friend Evelyn she didn't steal. And, mature for her age, she knew the meaning of privacy. Yes, Meena would be her protector.

Mr Goodridge arrived exactly two weeks after his letter. Fuller than his last photograph, he looked, to Leela, strong, vigorous and handsome. England was obviously good for him.

Clearly he hadn't lost his appetite. The meal she had prepared was wolfed down with such relish Mrs Goodridge didn't know whether to feel pleased or alarmed. Healthy and hungry, he was back, and she was sure she could detect a certain glint in his eyes that meant only one thing.

But he was tired from the long journey. That night he had held her gently by the shoulders and thanked her sincerely for the wonderful meal. Before retiring he had complimented her on the expansion of the store, kissed her on the left cheek and said, 'Goodnight Leela dear. You don't know how good it is to be home. You've done a wonderful job with the place, see you in the morning.'

Visitors came on Sunday. Old friends, Janice, Nancy, and children anxious for a glimpse of the man whose two uniformed portraits adorned the shop. Encouraged by their prompting, he whipped out his albums with photographs of his English 'mates' and West Indian friends. One album was dedicated to pictures of trains of various designs and from different angles, a 'Hoover' engine that travelled the Paddington to Birmingham route, and a close-up of 'the fast' from St Pancras to Luton. One photograph showed him posing with a cigarette, left foot atop a wooden chair, a thin circular mist rising above his felt hat. He looked sophisticated. She would have to watch out, Mrs Goodridge said to herself, he had become twice the man she married.

The visitors brought his favourite dishes and Alfred told his tales. Did they know, he asked an incredulous crowd one evening, that an ordinary needle from their store, if placed on the tracks, could derail an enormous monster of a train? Or that the leaves from any tree, green or dried, were so treacherous that men were paid to remove them from the railway line each dawn? A sharp intake of breath, murmurs of disbelief. And, he continued, did they know that he, Alfred Goodridge from Dubois, if he so wished, could bring the entire London rail service to gridlock by simply withholding permission for his train to leave the station?

Mrs Goodridge listened to his stories from her room, proud of his achievements and chuckling at the little additions with each fresh account. A good talker, the twelve years had given him the confidence to entertain an audience, the soft voice he had developed, and his gentle English accent, lending extra charm to each anecdote. With free drinks from the shop in return for their food and gifts, the visitors applauded his stories for the entire week, and still they wanted more.

Mrs Goodridge waited. Each night was going to be the dreaded night. But someone would ask for a repeat of a favourite episode, her husband would oblige, and she would fall sleep, another day ticked off the calendar.

Why had she got into such a state, she began to wonder, why had she made such a fuss, what was there to fear? Alfred was kind and gentle, with a comforting goodnight kiss and breakfast the moment she awoke; he did his share in the shop, allowing her to concentrate on her sewing. Understanding and sympathetic, he was like a new man.

On the afternoon of the Saturday of the second week, she heard her name being whispered.

'Leela, are you up?'

'Who, what?'

'Are you awake?'

'Um, yes.'

'Good, I have something to show you.'

'Oh my Lord.'

'It's a surprise, but I know you will like it.'

'Alfred, there's people in the shop and in the house.'

'It's not for them, it's for you.'

'Oh no.'

'You ready?'

'Give me a couple of minutes to wake up properly.'

'Hurry up Leela, I can't wait forever.'

'And another couple to brush me teeth.'

'All right.'

'And another five to fix me clothes.'

'Leela! Hurry!'

'Let me check where Meena is, Alfred, it's not fair on a young girl to have to go through this. Let me send her outside to play.'

'No need for that, Leela, there's no need for that.'

'Oh no, Alfred, you can't mean it: she is only a child and I have my pride.'

'Leave the girl out of this, it's between you and me.'

'Lord help me. Lord, find me another village to live. Find me a place where I can hide with my shame.'

'What's the matter with you, Leela, you never seen a man before?'

'Alfred, please! Dubois is a small place, St Vincent is only 100 square miles, my name will be all over the Grenadines. Please Alfred, please!'

Before she could finish her husband had marched into the room.

'Oh my Lord, Alfred!'

Leela uttered a loud gasp that brought Meena running to ask

if there was anything wrong. The young girl, too, was amazed.

'Mr Goodridge,' she asked, 'Mr Goodridge, that is really you?'

'Yes, it's me.'

'Can I touch it?'

'Yes, of course.'

'You can touch it too, you know, Leela, I've been looking forward to sharing it with you.'

'Alfred,' his wife said, approaching him with a pride that matched his, 'it's beautiful. It's wonderful, it really is you all over.'

'Thank you, Leela, I knew you would like it.'

'Those gold buttons, the belt, the shoes, the cap, they are magnificent,' the words were out before she could check herself, 'you don't know how they make me feel inside.'

That evening, Mrs Goodridge closed up the shop early.

'Alfred's tired,' she said to the customers, 'he needs a rest. Why don't you go home and read the newspapers or something? Janice and Nancy, it have calypso on the radio: you all don't like music?'

She had to see Alfred in his uniform again. Splendid, physical, confident, she felt like caressing him all over. His rich, grey moustache was strangely attractive, his stomach confirmed his stature as a man. For the first time in years she could see beyond the shop and sewing. Alfred in uniform had awoken her.

A shop in Penniston sold heavy cotton, she would make a suit like that for him if he insisted on returning to England. A week would be enough, she was sure of it. She drew the curtains, turned off the radio and shouted, 'Meena, why don't you go over to Evelyn to play hopscotch?'

At lunch the next day she said, 'Alfred, England is cold, isn't it?'

'Yes Leela. But you get accustomed to it.'

'You used to say the cold get right into your bones, is not time to come home?'

'Come home to what, Leela?'

'To the shop, to the village.'

'I can't give up my work, how will we live?'

'I could stretch my sewing and you can expand the shop, Alfred. People modern now, you know, they want new things and they have the money to pay.'

'But I'm a guard Leela, my work is important. Almost as important as the driver. Didn't you say how much you love the uniform?'

'But you can get a uniform-job here too: there's the police, the customs, I hear they even looking for men to join the army.'

'Do you think they will take me? Don't you think I'm a bit too old?'

'You, Alfred, old? I'm sure you're stronger than most of the men in Dubois. The fire brigade or police would be stupid to turn down a man like you.'

'Do you think so? Do you honestly think so Leela?'

'Honestly: you are still young and fit, you have overseas experience, you give off authority. To besides, no other man can carry off a uniform like you.'

taste for freedom

Damn codfish, blasted brown sugar that rot your teeth, evil white rum that scald your insides like black coffee straight off the coal pot: if you live on Prescott Estate that is the reward for your labour.

Seven hours chopping cane or clearing bush, driving back idle white snake, sun beating down on man, woman and child, and when Friday come, what? A rough bundle with your pay, a old crocus bag to sling over your shoulder! Same size bag for Mervyn Greaves who work like he possessed, and for that weakling Ezekiel Hollis who faint if his foot touch a frog. Out before the sun wash her face, back when she tired, that is the way we live. All that suppose to change, but change slower than Mr Prescott lame white horse.

The new law give one hour for breakfast but by ten o'clock the sun so hot, shade more important than chocolate-tea and bread.

Sun eating the clothes off your back, you sleep and rest rather than eat. You can't help it. Cropping sugar cane hard, the leaf cut through your shirt sleeve, graze your elbow and slice the skin below your knee. Where the cane tall your face and neck always wounded.

Every day, come rain, come shine, every day except Sunday, the same thing. Your foot hurt, the shoulder tighten, your back knot up so much you can't touch your toes unless you sit down. And Mr Prescott still paying we, grown man and woman, in saltfish, herring, mackerel, white rum and brown sugar!

Pay suppose to come in hard money, in coins you could roll between your fingers and smell. A man arrive here some months back. Short and stumpy, he from the Caddy Estate in Dauphin, we find out after he leave. Thirty shillings in his pocket, nobody know his business, even his name he keep secret.

The word get around so men and men gather by the rain-tree near Peter Ryan house at seven o'clock to see real money. And I in the middle, watching this man, eyeing him up good-good. He black the same as me, probably a couple years younger. But he have one thing over me and all the workers on Prescott Estate: he get real money for his labour. Although he can't more than twenty-five, he could see what he working for, his pay don't end up in a scratch hole in a banana field.

The man, Dauphin, we call him, leave the same way he arrive. One day he here, the next gone. Back to Dauphin? Nobody could tell. As usual we turn up in the evening with peanuts, mango, breadfruit, cassava bread and breadnut for a peep or a play with the coins. A little boy, one of Ima Steven grandson there too, I don't know who invite him. Carrying two pretty ground doves for the stranger, he stand there small and proud. For a glimpse of real money, to touch a coin, he risk a beating from the big men and women he insult with his short-pants company.

Later, on the way home we talk about the youth; he bold, we agree, he have spirit. He know already what we, tough old men and women, just finding out: a man must able to do what he please with his pay. A woman too. With round shillings and pence in your hand your pay is yours to save or squander. But food and drink for toil? What kind of meal on this earth you could make with white rum and herring?

We not guests at Mr Prescott table. Where we have name like Nanton, Fergus, Ellis, Williams and Riley, they go by De Santos, Ollivere, Dauphin, Warner, Arnison and Caddy. Big-name people, they bawling that they poor now. The money the British government give them not enough, the sugar hogshead down, field workers staying off sick for spite.

They careful to bawl in the night when they think we asleep or when they believe the house-servants not listening. But some of the servants smarter than they realise. They watch and hear, they learn quick-quick. They bow, serve and smile, 'Thank you, sir, thank you madam,' but they listen and notice. And when Mr Prescott drunk, or when he go to bed early, Nancy Herbert 'borrow' his newspaper and books for me and my friend, Cyril Nero.

The Childs, Dauphins, Ollivere, Warren, Ryan and the Forbes, who use to stylish and lordy-lady, feeling it, Nancy pinch me and whisper. Born the same year, same month, three days part me and Nancy; since we small we walking out. Watch Mrs Prescott good, she tell me, see if her step don't change, watch her good-good.

And she not the only one. When the white people pass us now they see our face, they tear open their eyes like we strangers from a next village or like they seeing us for the first time. Their English walk slow down so much, Nancy whisper, if you see them from behind, or if they cover their face from the heat, you realise they born under the sun too.

Some of the bounce gone out their step for truth, but real hard time don't really meet them; confuse by what happen a year ago, they walk round like everything they possess might wash into the sea when it rain in the mountains and the river come down.

You can't blame them. Give up sweet life, pretty cotton dress and expensive suit from England, say goodbye to dancing and brandy? No master! No mistress! So they hang on to old times. Every month they still have their big feast and dance like the world about to end. Fowl, roast pig and stew beef still plenty on their table, with hot white yam, sweet potato, tannia, dasheen and peas; champagne still flow after their passion fruit, guava juice and ginger beer.

Little as I own I don't jealous them. They have their life, we have our own. But I pray that Mr Prescott serve them one night what we get every Friday pay day. See how they like it. Let them see how much different meal they could make with herring and bony dry cod that rotten round the edge.

A fellow with my taste, a man who could name lemon-grass, mint, garlic, lavender, pineapple, thyme, any herb on the estate, a man who could smash a cocoa pod, suck the seed and tell you how many days till it truly ripe, a man who know fruit like bird know them, and they asking me to eat fish that catch months ago in some damn place over the sea!

Blasted codfish, since when fish need extra salt? They spend their whole life in the sea, so why they want a extra coat of salt, they keeping away magic spell or evil spirit or something? And if cod or herring not to your taste, what you going to do with them, throw them to the mangy dogs that roam the village?

So much fish in the river. Mullet the length of your arm, grouper, sandfish, lobster and crayfish. Broad-mouth suckstone you could see from the bridge before you turn left to go to Jennings Mountain, swim about without a care in the world, getting fatter and fatter each day. By the edge of the river where the current weak, conger eel sleep at six in the evening and pray you don't chop them with your cutlass on the way home after work.

River fish, little one, big one, dirty-brown, black, shiny, blue-and-yellow, if you have the time you could stand by the bridge and just gaze at them. Nothing beautiful so. But when it rain in the mountain and Yambou river come down it fling them, big and small, onto the river bank. Wriggling to get back into the water is a sad-sad sight. Poor things, we feel sorry for them, real sorry. Cause they going to end up in our pot! I believe they know that: fish have a sad face that make me think they understand that they belong in a broth, that they only swimming about in Yambou until their time come.

To a man like me who learn the art of taste, nothing could beat a fish broth. A peg of garlic, a little pepper and a pinch of salt and you really in things. You mustn't get fancy with fish. Salt, dasheen-leaf, a hand of bananas or a young breadfruit make a meal fit for any man or woman.

'Why you don't allow we a change of diet,' Cyril ask Mr

Prescott one Tuesday morning some months back, 'why you don't let us use the river? Crayfish go well with callaloo and young bananas, why you prevent we from catch them?'

Mr Prescott like to tell his big friends how he a patient man, how he treat his workers the best on the leeward coast. With my own ears I hear him boast how 'my people' content, how we just like his own children. But I could see he don't take to Cyril suggestion. Like all the white men on the estate he don't care for people who could read, talk or ask question. *They* should talk, *we* must listen. And those who don't hear will feel, as one of the overseer, Hilton Hadley, the evilest man who ever ride a black horse, like to say when we cutting cane.

Cyril big and strapping, with a neck the size of the trunk of a coconut tree, so they careful not to cross him. He talk his mind, who vex vex. After he take in what Cyril ask him Mr Prescott take off his black felt hat, doll back his brown hair like me and Cyril is woman he want to impress, and cock his left foot upon a stone. We just crossing Hope River to go to Jennings Valley to cut cane that morning and Mr Prescott walking his dogs.

'Cyril Nero,' he say, like he delivering sermon, 'I know you have plenty mouth, I know you could run the estate better than me. Since those interfering Moravians taught you and your friends to read, write and reckon, you think you know everything about everything. Well, let me tell you this: when you have your own land, when you have your own river, then you could catch fish. Before that time comes, you take what I give you and keep away from Yambou.'

'But the river not yours, Mr Prescott, is God river,' Cyril reply.

'The river flows through my land so it's mine.'

'God make the river, God make the sea, he make them for everybody.'

'Who put that idea into your head?'

'What idea?'

'About God and the river.'

'Nobody have to tell me that, is nature.'

'Well let *me* tell *you* this: the river belongs to the estate, you hear me?'

'Well tell God that.'

'What was that?'

'Tell God that. And watch your hat.'

For just at that moment the dogs take off into the banana field barking like they spot a agouti and Mr Prescott get ready to follow them. At the top of the bank where the field begin, he turn round to give Cyril a bad eye and wag his finger. Cyril smile back like he forming a kiss to blow, we dip our cutlass in the river to clean them, and Mr Prescott disappear into the banana field behind the dogs.

Emancipation come just over a year ago. A small white man from down the coast arrive one evening with a letter and ask everyone to gather round.

From far he look like the Moravian who used to teach me, Nancy and Cyril to read the Bible and newspaper, and to count. When we finish lessons, he used to ask the names of the plants and herbs we use in cooking and, in a little book he keep in his pocket, he write them down. When I reach closer I see it wasn't Festus Frank. This man have a long narrow face and coarse ginger hair, as though he stay out in the sun too long and it turn his hair for spite. A big crowd form. The man look like a child with so much people circle him but he don't lose himself. Like he accustom to black people, big crowd don't seem to bother him. He wait for quiet, then he look down at his paper and begin.

'The letter I'm holding,' he say, 'gives you freedom. From August the first, you're free to set up your own home, you're free to cultivate your own gardens. You can grow your own crops, you can rear pigs, goats and chickens. That is the law. You are no longer apprentices, you are to become your own men and women. Nobody could force you to work now. If you want, you could up and go somewhere else and live.'

Before people could get too excited, when he notice people looking at one another, he hold up his right hand for attention again.

'You're free to go to any part of the island,' he continue, 'but I suggest that you stay where you were born and where you grew up, among people you know and trust. You will hear lots of stories about other places, you will do well not to pay them any attention.'

He talk for over an hour, we listen in silence. All set of law, rule and suggestion he read out. Too much to take in, we get some of the words but lose most. The evening hot, but even with the heat, surround by so much strange face, he never stumble once. Is as if he learn what he going to say and only keep the paper close by in case he miss out a little detail.

He take his time, read out rule and law, law and rule. Then he roll up the paper and ask how many people on the estate could read. Five of us, Nancy, Cyril, me, Mingo Francis and Mella Myall, used to take lessons from the Moravians and 'borrow' Mr Prescott's books. The best reader, Nancy hand go up first.

'Take this letter,' he say in trembling voice, 'read it to the people. Tell them that they are free, but remind them of their responsibilities also. Now, I will take questions.'

Workers don't ask English and Portuguese people anything, so no one sure what to say. Mr Prescott have a way he look at anybody who put question to him, his moon-face tighten when you say something he don't like, so most people burn their thinking in their mouth. Cyril is the only man who ask him, 'Why?' and tell him, 'No'. This small white man in a black suit and neat black tie smile and put his right hand on Arthur Price shoulder like he want us know that he not in with Mr Prescott. Still nobody want to be first to put a question to him. Everybody expect Cyril to say something but he find Nancy and they going through the letter.

'What going to happen to my children,' Margery Clarke ask when she see that nobody going to say anything, 'they could stop work just like that?'

'Yes, the law will protect them.'

'Is true if you have the money,' Martha Morgan join in, 'you could buy a piece of land?'

'Land is expensive, but if you work hard and learn the art of saving, there are no limits to what you can do. You have the opportunity to control your future. Don't believe for a minute that it will be easy, but if you follow what I've just said, you will learn the true meaning of freedom.'

Talking among themself the crowd start to leave few moments later. What the white man say make them think hard, and the best place to consider is always at home in your own cottage.

'Go to church and thank the merciful Lord for your freedom,' he say as the crowd thin out, 'go to church and don't give in to sin and earthly temptations.'

The day before the fateful day, we follow his advice. In twos and threes adults march down to the river, children the four miles to the sea at Mount Bentick. July-August weather, the river cold, the sea blue-and-green, with white swell racing each other to the shore, rolling and breaking on top one another like two of Cyril dogs playing. We bathe and wash the mud and sweat from our body. The women wash each other hair, men use dry coconut husk or vine to wash their own skin and hair, dive, wash again, then stay for minutes under the cold water.

Quiet we march down to the sea and river, quieter we walk back home. The day still as a Sunday and hot, a long afternoon after a ten-hour morning. Dress in our best clothes, we cook Sunday food, fowl for those who rear them, corned pork, or fish from Yambou. Some force themself to eat, but for most the food remain in the pot on the fire stones. Out in the mud road, away from our wattle-and-daub, we empty and hungry but we full. The new life they promise take away our appetite. Nobody know what to expect so we laugh and joke to cover up our fears.

Hot and sweaty, a hundred banana leaf fanning, the church at Magum open from seven. Women pack the inside, children and men listen through the windows. Some people cry, some sob-sing, others keep their head down, quiet with their thinking. We listen to scripture, chant 'Amen' and 'Thank you Lord' and try to carry on like is just another day.

Joining hands, we pray for ourself and our children, we ask to get on with our neighbour. In the warm night we hug each other, big and little, friend and enemy, boy and girl, man and woman.

Crickets tweep, mad fowl crow as if morning already arrive. But after so many years we know how to be patient. We pray for the old, the weary and the sick who stay in their bed, glad of a extra day of rest, we pray for the children to come after us and their children. Then is time to go. Just before midnight, in a light drizzle, we walk home, slow, in silence, to wait for August 1st.

Emancipation come, we free, according to the law. Nancy read out the letter on the day, people listen, we try to explain while we ourself try to understand . Things going to change, things *have* to change.

Prescott Estate used to have thirty-four family before emancipation, a few months after, they count thirty-three. Five family pick up and head for Vermont where they hear life easy, two just grab their bundle and take to the road. Thirty-four family, five gone, then two, how that make thirty-three? Simple. Like the whole island on the move! Some curious to see what happening on other estates, some want a change of neighbour, the stink and noise of the village drive the rest away. Anywhere that promise a fair wage they making for. So seven family move out, but six move in.

One of the new family go straight to Prescott. This family quiet, close, they nod 'Hello', but they serious-serious, no time to stop and talk. I don't know if they have some kind of letter, perhaps they meet Mr Prescott when he travel to another estate. Anyway, the family, man, wife and two scrawny children, spend nearly two hours in the big house.

With one of the largest estate in Charlotte Parish, Prescott don't normally allow black people in his home. Servant and maid do the cooking and cleaning, and Augustus Pebbles walk the horse when Prescott wake up late or drunk, but no other black foot wipe on his mat. The Prescotts don't come into our home, and we not welcome in theirs. In the open under the sky is where we talk. What this man and his wife have over the people who rear up here, we ask one another?

Next day before the sun properly wake up we find out: the family offer Prescott five pounds and, swift as a doctor-bird, he sell them two acres of flat land by the river. The land stony but, as Nancy say, stone or stone-not, land is land, not true? Your own house on your own land: that is the only way to live. Prescott hard up for money, Cyril say later that day, when we coming home from cutting cane, Prescott getting poor, that is why he sell. Once upon a time, the biggest English man in the parish would have shame to take money from a slave hand!

So is one big movement since emancipation. Things better down the leeward side, windward people feel, life must easier round the corner or over the hill.

But the old, the weary and the proud choose to stay. New overseers, new faces, not for them, better to stay than have to come back and die of shame. Then one day is my turn to leave. One Tuesday morning I just slip away easy-easy. No one hear or see me, just Nancy and Cyril know I take off with my Georgie-bundle to get my own land.

I leave the estate but I have nowhere in mind. Prescott trap my spirit too long, is time to set it free. But when I reach the main road a problem hit me: Left else right, which way to turn? Twenty-five years and I never properly set foot outside the estate grounds! Big-big me, Joel Morgan, and I only see one patch of sky!

Elephant, tiger, monkey and alligator might live alongside people in Richland Park, Richmond and Ribishi; for all I know, the people in those village might be blue, green, or black like we, they could white down the left side and black down the right: we never see them and they don't know us. If the leeward coast have white sand and the river flow from the sea to the mountain, I going to find out before Nancy and Cyril.

At the main road, then, with my problem, I spit in my left palm like I see some fellows do, chop the spit in two with my big finger and note the direction where most go. Was left, so I go left, simple as that. That is how I end up in the mountains.

The road don't take me direct to the mountains, if you could call the road a road. No bigger than a track, it dirty, brown-and-red with fresh mud, and stony, with corner upon corner, and still more corner after that.

I go round one tight corner, another one waiting for me. This is road for donkey-cart and horse, animals you could train, animals that don't heed direction but obey when you say 'Stop'. My bare foot slipping and sharp stone chooking, I keep walking through the mud, past Petit Bordel, past Byahaut, Frenches and Gomea, until I come to Akers.

The sea on my left, the mountains on the right, I never realise the island so beautiful. The sea blue and calm, the mountain high and green with white cloud sleeping on top. It so pretty here, right near where we grow up, and it take twenty-five years to find out!

Everywhere green-looking and healthy with wide, deep-green banana leaf longer than Nancy skirt, lime tree, groundnut field full of tiny doves, coconut, bamboo and cocoa trees. Away from the muddy road, on top hill so steep I wonder how people manage to stand up straight to plant and reap them, row upon row of corn, tannia bank, onion and dasheen. One day, I promise myself, piece of this land will be mine. Gazing like a child, looking left and right, I walk on, taking my time. I don't know where I going but once is away from Prescott Estate, fine.

A few travellers pass me, a family of five with their everything in a little bundle on their head or in a small ping-wing basket, a man with a shiny cutlass in his hand, a woman dragging two children faster than their little feet could manage. 'Morning,' they say, with their head down, as though they in a hurry to beat the sun. 'Morning,' I answer from my dream, 'good morning.' The people going in the other direction nod and go about their business. Where they heading I don't ask because, if they put the same question to me, what I going to tell them?

Stop and take a rest, my body suggest after four barefoot hours in the mud and stone, rest now, set out again when it cooler. I turn off at the track to the next village, carry on for about ten minutes, then obey my tired legs. The first breadfruit tree I come to, at the mouth of the village, tall and wide with enough shade for a family of six. I rest down my tiny bundle, place the cutlass carefully next to it, and sit between the fat grey roots of the tree.

Never out of season, breadfruit don't let you down, Nancy like to say; you could roast it, cook it, boil the bush for head-cold, or drink it warm with a little sugar or molasses. A half-ripe one she roast yesterday for the journey sitting sweet in my basket. Thank goodness for the breadfruit tree I say to myself, as I stretch out between the roots, thank you Captain Bligh.

The sun just warming up before she really start shine, so I figure is about ten o'clock, breakfast time back in Prescott. A piece of breadfruit and a half-ripe mango is my first meal as a man. I chew slow, wondering if I do the right thing. But you have to obey your spirit, you have to learn to walk alone. Land don't come to those comfortable in another man home.

I sit in the shade under the tree eating and wondering. The village quiet, too quiet. It take a while before I realise is Tuesday morning, everyone at work except children too young to go to the fields. The law save and protect them, so they spend their day idle. Half hour later the sun break through the shade of the tree and, tired from the journey, I drop off.

When I wake up the sun ruling the sky. Prescott noisy from cock-crow to night, this village silent like a burial ground. I shake the sleep out my clothes, drag myself up and begin to wander about. The houses rude and damp, ugly, I soon see, wattle-and-daub halfway between round and square. Heavy rain must peel away the outside the same way it treat my little brown mud cottage in Prescott, I say to myself, is a sin to live like that.

I stop to pick a guava from a tree by the road. Two muddy children sitting on a branka shout me.

'Aye man, what your name?' a girl about twelve ask.

I turn to look at them and continue eating the guava.

'Where you from?' the girl continue, like she really want to know.

'Prescott,' I say, 'I from Prescott.'

'Where that be?'

'Over there,' I say pointing to the east, 'over that hill and the next one.'

'What it like there?' the boy ask.

'Dirty, muddy, just like this village.'

'Somewhere else like Montrose?'

'Every place like Montrose!'

'My father cutting cane,' the girl say, 'why you not working, you finish your task for today?'

'I leave the estate,' I reply, 'I give up working on Prescott.'

'How you going get money?'

'None of your damn business!'

'You looking for somebody?' the boy ask, 'you have family in Montrose?'

'No, I don't have family and I don't know anybody in Montrose.'

'Is Norma Cobbler he come to see,' the girl say to the boy, and they both burst out laughing.

' Norma Who?' I ask.

They laugh again and I feel stupid because I don't know what they find funny.

'You don't know Norma?' the boy say, 'everybody know Norma.'

'Except me,' I reply.

'Then something had was to wrong with you.'

'Norma-man,' the girl continue, 'Sammy say if he could touch your cutlass.'

'If you want touch a cutlass wait till your father come home,' I bark, 'go and bathe your muddy self and don't bother me!'

Soon as I walk away from them I feel evil, like a man born old or one who forget his boy-days and children games. But somehow my spirit don't take to the place: the children don't have manners and they ask too much hard question. Even the yellow hibiscus and red dragon blood in the tiny gardens, the ripe plum and mango smell, the bananas fulling on every plot of land, can't turn me. Montrose set in a valley, a hill block the sea, rain water settle everywhere you turn, mud come up to your ankle. How my spirit could take to a second village like Prescott?'

I walk through the village, slow, stepping over puddle, past dog and cat and chickens scratching in the mud for worms. Coconut shell, rotting mango, banana skin and cane peel cover the little track through the village. Flies go from shell to mango seed to banana skin to cane peel. Hundred upon hundred, noisy and nasty, they take off when I get close, and return to feed soon as I pass. Rising from a tiny cottage on my right, where three girls roasting plantains, the smoke burn my eyes. This place is a hole. I walk quickly through, shoo-ing the flies, chasing stray cat and dog and never looking back. After a short time I end up in the mountains.

Green and tall, in another year the mountain trees bound to reach the clouds. From their leaf high-high above, rain water plop on my bare head and clothes.

Nowhere to hide from the rain or to block out the strange sounds. 'Monkey Eric, Monkey Eric,' a parrot singing wherever I go, 'Monkey Eric, Monkey Eric.' The rain, unfamiliar sounds and darkness make me wish I back in my little muddy cottage with the cockroach, scorpion and centipede that hide in my clothes and under the fire stones. At night, when it dark and quiet, when snake, owl and lizard searching for food, I pull a crocus bag over my head and wonder what I doing here when I already have a cottage. But a wattle-and-daub too shaky in the rainy season: solid mahogany is my dream.

Three days it take to get use to the birds, pigs, goats, lizards and wild animals that live here. Three days before vines stop trip me up, before I find the trees that keep out the rain.

All the while I feel the mountain watching me the same way I used to watch the fish in the river. When it ready, I feel sure, it going to treat me like I treat the mullet, suckstone and grouper in Yambou. The vines going to trap me, wrap themselves round my body, and squeeze the blood out of me, or the clouds going to come down and stifle me when I in a tree-top picking fruits.

Yet I feel happy here, free, I think I could stay. I have to stay, I can't live in Montrose and only a man without shame could go back to Prescott. So I cut down twelve bamboo, stake them in the ground and gather ping-wing and wide banana leaf. Some smaller leaf to weave in between to keep out rain and, by Saturday night, I have a little house!

Sunday I wake up at twelve, eat a bit of breadfruit, read a chapter from a book Nancy 'borrow' from Mr Prescott library, then go back to sleep. Monday to Wednesday, to draw out my food, the same. Muddy, dirty and stink from houses so close you could push over your neighbour latrine, even though hunger killing me, I don't miss Prescott. The stink, the noise and the fat chiggers that plant themself into your toes or your bottom-foot; blind cockroach that fly into your pot in the evening; the centipede and scorpion that creep up and sting, let them stay there, I happy here, even though I on my own.

In a dream Friday night I show Nancy my little bamboo house. The smile on her face! She have long fingers and neat, pretty toes. I play with her fingers till she sigh soft and close her eyes. When I reach down for her toes the dream end. On Sunday the codfish in my basket finish, the breadfruit and the cassava as well, hungry really catching up with me. Next time Nancy see me she might see a spirit.

Agouti, wild fowl, manicou, pig, iguana and rabbit wandering about the mountain but I never the kind of man who like food that give trouble. I see the fowl and iguana during the day, renking manicou I smell at night.

Agouti that fraid it own shadow bold here; catch me, they say, try and see if you can catch me. But I know better. You could chase a tiny agouti for ten minutes and, unless you make it go downhill, you always lose. With those short front legs it can race up a bank, but if you get it running down a gully you have a chance. Me chase young agouti? No master, no mistress!

Fowl clever and swift, manicou and iguana sly like mongoose. Like I say, I don't like trouble-food. Climb wet tree to catch manicou and iguana? Chase fowl that flatter and then fly off? Who, me?

I miss the taste of beef, the pork we get once a month, and the fowl Cyril rear in his yard. But all I can do now is remember those Sundays. I could catch a fowl, a fat iguana or a slow manicou, I tell myself, I can do it! But after the effort is another hour to skin, clean, and season them with onion, chive and garlic the way I like it. And that is before you start a fire to cook! Lord, I have to find a way to eat soon.

Cyril have the skill for fire. Nancy show him. They know where to find the dry wood, straw and grass, they know how to cover the baby fire with their palm to make it grow. I don't have it. Ten times Nancy show me, ten times I fail. I rub and rub till my fingers burn but the fire still don't light. I can't light a fire, and mountain animals don't give me a chance. Only one thing left, fruit.

At first I stick to the fruits I know good, plumrose, banana, fig and mango. Mango become my flesh. And is new flesh every day: dibique, turpentine, parlover, horsey, hairy-cat and purple scuttle that so pretty is a shame to eat them. But you can't eat codfish every Friday, same with mango, no matter how smooth and sweet.

Birds good to follow, I find out when I get tired of mango, they know the mountain best. From up high they see everything and take what they need. Bird only share with bird, they fly out together and come home in a flock. To learn their secret I watch them same as I use to watch mysterious Dauphin.

They notice me back, they behave like they know me good. Flying over Prescott, Dauphin, Childs, and all the other estates on the island, they see how we live all these years, no place secret from them. When they find the right spot they fly off to feed. I track them, find the place, eat what they eat then return to my bamboo home.

Mango, soursop, guava and pineapple, they peck away and, when their tiny belly empty, they fly back for more. If a flock land on a tree, eat till they full, I reason is safe to do the same. I study the birds close, smell, then taste, the fruits they feed on. When they go to a village too far away, I wish I have wings to go with them.

One afternoon they lead me into Keartons, to a stout tree with round brown-skin fruit high up on the neck. On the ground by the roots, about a dozen fruits that fall during the night. The smell! Is like a turpentine mango mix with warm molasses. The birds peck away like is their first meal for three days. Locking the fruit with their claw, head bobbing up and down, is as if they dancing to music as they move round it to feed. To get a taste I have to shoo them away with my cutlass.

I feel the fruit. The brown skin tougher than the birds make it look. I twist till the stem loose, then drop three of them careful on the ground and quick-quick I slide down the tree for my turn.

With my cutlass I chop open the roundest and biggest one and slice it. The smell, that mad smell: it remind me of how I feel when it raining hard during the night and Nancy close to me. Like a raven child I stuff three slices into my mouth. Uhmmmmm. The flesh more gold than yellow and tight, no wonder the birds love it. Uhmmmmm. I reach for another slice.

The first bite into this slice I begin to feel dizzy. My head start to spin, I fall flat on my back like the morning Cyril donkey kick me in the stomach. Lying on the ground, my stomach knot up, my hands tremble and my legs cramp. What happen after that I don't remember. When I wake up the moon shining bright. I curse the fruit, make a note of the tree and mark the place.

Luck roll with me from that afternoon: a green hairy fruit swell my belly for three days, a single red berry make me so drowsy one afternoon it take a night to catch myself. After that, no more fruit-trouble. I learn from the birds, use smell before taste and leave strange fruit where they belong. Every leaf and fruit I eat I keep in my head. All the nuts in the mountain I try, none disagree with me. Two months after I leave Prescott, when I know all the fruits, nuts and plants in this part of the mountain, I remember it need hard money to buy land, so I decide to find the nearest village.

I go on a Sunday, two o'clock, lunch over, people resting before work the next day. Montrose alive. Most people glad to get out of their little wattle-and-daub, a few sitting by the door cooling off, their mud floor drying in the breeze. Under the shade of a rain tree a woman selling sugar cake in a tray; next to her a son with raw peanuts on a crocus bag.

Buying, selling or just wandering about, nobody know me, but nobody take notice. I find a shady spot under a mapoo tree and set down my basket of mountain goods. Soon a little crowd gather. They point at the fruits, turn to one another and tear their eye like they seeing a spirit. They want to buy but they afraid. I bite into a yellow, ripe hog-plum, chew, spit out the seed, and swallow the flesh. Those close by hold out their hand for one like naughty children for licks. They smell it, suck it, bite it and then chew with half a mouth. In less than a time all the hog-plum gone. The damsel, grape, fat pork, gum cherry, pineapple and plumrose soon follow.

A big crowd waiting for me the next Sunday when I arrive with my tray-load of plumrose, pineapple, turpentine mango and tamarind. They braver now, they trust me. I sell fruit and they pass over hard money.

The months pass. Every Sunday I bringing something different for my little crowd under the mapoo tree. They taste, ask the name, put in their order for this fruit and agree the price. Montrose Estate pay in shillings so my money rising. Plenty small make big, I tell myself on the way home, one-one full up the boli. When I stretch out on the floor of my mountain house I see a nice piece of land waiting for me and Nancy, and a cottage not from bamboo but from solid mahogany.

Early one Sunday when I reach the village another fellow selling fruit under my tree. I curse the ground he walking on and

swear at him for thiefing my living. Walkback Charlie is a tall
fellow, much taller than me, with long arms and a straight back
and a busy walk. He like to smile plenty, and when he notice me
he grin like he catch me in a banana field on top his sister
yesterday.

'You in my spot,' I tell him.

'My spot in the ground, your spot there too.'

'Go somewhere else, move your business.'

'Move my what?'

'Your tray. Move it.'

'Who say?'

'I say.'

'And who are you?'

' Don't bother about that, just move.'

'Is bad you bad so?'

'No, I'm not bad but you in my place, go find your own.'

'Plenty mapoo tree in the village.'

'So find one.'

'But I like this one. It shady, it cool, it get a good sea breeze.'

'The spot belong to me, Walkback Charlie, if you don't move
your tray, you don't sell another fig in Montrose.'

'All right, all right, but I tell you what, why we don't taste for
it? You bring all kind of funny fruit to sell, why we don't *taste* for
the spot?'

'How you mean?'

'You bring five things, I bring five, I taste yours, you taste
mine. If mine make you throw up, I win. If yours work my belly,
you win.'

'What you know about fruit? You find some mangy-looking

passion fruit somewhere, you have mango that even dog will refuse and you call yourself a fruit-man?'

'When we have the taste I will show you who is the *real* fruit-man. I am a mountain-man, you know, I spend a whole two weeks in Mespo mountain eating nothing but fruit. I will work your belly till you bawl for your mother like a baby!'

'What about some meat,' I suggest, 'why we don't throw in some meat?'

'Anything you want Joel Morgan. Anything you have I can better.'

'Next Sunday,' I say, 'this Sunday coming?'

'This coming Sunday.'

'Sunday, then.'

I leave my tray with a small boy, Prince, who there waiting for me every Sunday and who always the last to leave. Sell what left, I tell him, and keep the money. Walkback Charlie bold and bareface but I can't underrate him, I have to prepare myself. And if luck with me, that same Walkback Charlie going to build my home.

Back in my little bamboo house in the mountain, I sit down and wonder what to give him. With so much fruits to choose from I have to win. I can't lose my living, I promise Nancy house and land, I can't live with shame. Tangerine, orange, mango, he bound to know, plumrose, guava and fig give themselves away with their smell. What to use, what fruit to tie him up with, and what meat?

A voice appear in my head later that day. 'Give him the fruits you take to the village,' it tell me, 'surprise him with simple fruit. As for meat, make that simple too, simple fruit, easy meat.'

The 'taste Sunday', Montrose swell with people. Everyone dress up in their best clothes, men in white cotton shirt and pants that reach just below the knee, women in long white dresses and headties. The children I see walking about with their face, hand and leg caked with mud, shiny and clean that morning. Smelling of the coconut oil on every part of their body, they look new as if they just fall from the sky. Under every tree groundnut cake, coconut water and potato pudding for sale. Drinking, talking, standing about, people waving and shouting to their neighbour like they in the next village, not a donkey-kick away.

With my tray I make my way to the house we agree. Mother Howe come out to meet me. A *Mother* in the local Baptist church, she is the chief judge.

'Joel Morgan, people bet their hard-earn money,' she say, loosening a string around her waist and taking out a bag of coins from under her long white dress, 'I want a fair taste, I hope you don't bring poison fruit.'

'No, Mother Howe, is just mountain fruit I have.'

'Good.'

She take me to a room in her mahogany house and check my tray and meat bowl.

'How you want the fruit prepare?' she ask.

'Eat the first four, boil the last one,' I tell her. 'What Walkback Charlie have?'

'You know I can't tell you that. But *he* have good fruit, *you* have good fruit.'

'What about meat?'

'*He* have a good stew, *your* broth good too.'

Mother Howe have two judges to help, one for me, one for

Walkback Charlie. My judge take my meat bowl and place it on a fire by the door next to Walkback Charlie meat bowl. Then Mother Howe and the judges lead me outside through the back door. Walkback Charlie already there. He stare at me and I stare him back. He smile that smile again, but it don't reach a grin this time. I smile like I catch him leaving a load in a scratch hole in a banana field.

When a fight going to break out a crowd have a way about it: nobody want to see blood, but they feel you cheat them if they don't see solid blows. That is how it feel: like a big fight, only sitting down, for nearly a hundred people. The judges take out two blindfolds as Mother Howe read out the rules.

'Walkback Charlie, Joel Morgan, eat and drink quiet.'

'Yes, Mother Howe.'

'Once the taste start, you don't ask question, you mustn't talk.'

'Yes, Mother Howe.'

' If you get up off your stone you lose.'

'Yes, Mother Howe.'

'You have three minutes to finish each fruit. Take more than that and you lose.'

'Yes, Mother Howe.'

'The first one to bring up anything, lose.'

'Yes, Mother Howe.'

'Good.'

The two judges put on the blindfolds. My man draw mine so tight it almost cover my nose.

'Ready?' Mother Howe ask.

'Ready.'

'First taste,' Mother Howe give the order.

I stretch out my left hand and my judge place a fruit in it. A large sugar-apple, the mouldy smell and the softness give it away. I peel it careful, suck on the fleshy pegs and draw out the seeds with my tongue. I keep the dozen seeds in my right hand till I finish, then pass them to the judge. All this time I hear Walkback Charlie cracking the tamarind pod, my fruit, and then sucking at the flesh. A loud cheer after two minutes tell me he manage to eat the sharp tamarind without much bother.

His second is a sapodilla, soft and sweet to make you sick, a fruit Nancy adore but I hate. I peel away the skin, eat the soft flesh and pray that Walkback don't have another sapodilla on his tray. One I could take, two edge my teeth. So if he have another, I in big-big trouble. As I force down the sapodilla, I hear him sucking, chewing and cleaning his teeth to get rid of the hairs from the 'hairy-cat' mango, my second fruit. From the sucking, grunting and spitting, he sound irritated. Good, I say to myself, mango working!

The number three is his 'big stick', I know that as soon as the judge pass me a cup and ask me to drink. I take the cup up to my nose, slow, to get the smell. Aloes can't hide. People use it to wash their skin and hair, to clear their stomach and to put on cut and bruise. The bitterness hard to take but I drink the first dose slow, get my stomach ready, then finish off the rest in one go. It turn my stomach but the sweetness of the sapodilla help keep it down. A hog plum I bring to Montrose many times is the third from my tray. As I expect, Walkback Charlie eat it without a problem.

Clapping break out.

'Charlie!,' a woman voice scream out, 'Walkback Charlie.'

'Charlie,' a male voice join in, ' Charlie!'

'Joel Morgan,' Prince respond, 'Mister Morgan!'

Under the blindfold all the things I could have give him start to run through my mind: dung-cane to swell his mouth, dry juice to send him crazy with one sip, gumcherry to stick his lips together and slow him down.

The chant make me begin to worry. Suppose my big stick don't work? Suppose he stronger than he look? Take it easy, I tell myself, you have the thing for him, don't worry. For fruit four he serve a half-ripe pawpaw, I have a overripe soursop: both of we still sitting.

I start to worry again. What happen if my big stick can't break him? Suppose Charlie stomach strong? He big, he tall, he spend time in the mountains like me: what happen if he as good as he say? The crowd hot up again, Prince shout my name, three or four cheer for Walkback Charlie.

'Last fruit,' Mother Howe tell the crowd, 'last one.'

The crowd hush again. I wonder what Walkback Charlie save up for last. Whatever he have, I tell myself, I could better. A mountain man, a man who learn from birds, a man who fruit knock out three times and three times he get up, whatever he have, I have something stronger, whatever he offer I have the head and stomach for it.

'Serve the fruit,' Mother Howe order the judges.

A fat plantain is Walkback Charlie last shot. Cousin to banana, it thick and tough when green but when ripe you can boil or roast it and make a good meal with a bit of pork or even codfish. This plantain green. I take a tiny bite from one end, chew and try to swallow. The flesh taste of stain, it bitter, is like eating wood mix with sand. No way I could finish it in three minutes if I eat it like a ripe banana or a fig. I take two quick big bites, half-chew, and swallow. A thousand ants crawling about in my stomach, I have to get them out, I have to get them out!

But just when I forcing to keep the plantain down I hear a rumbling noise.

'Eeeeuuuuuh,' Walkback Charlie cry out, 'Eeeeuuuuuh!'

'Walkback Charlie,' Mother Howe say, 'no noise, that is the rule.'

'Euuuuuuh!'

'You getting up?'

'Euuhh!'

'Then keep it down: you must not bring anything up. Understand?'

'Euh.'

'Charlie!'

'Eu.'

A cure for cold, headache and fever, wild onion renk until. The smell alone make sick children get better immediately. But just as I think the wild onion going to make him give in Walkback manage to control his stomach. He tough, he tough for truth.

'Bring out the meat bowls,' Mother Howe order the judges, 'fifteen shillings for the man who still sitting!'

The crowd go silent again. Real hush now, the moment come. I hear the sound of the lid coming off the bowls. I stretch out both hands and take mine.

Charlie bowl have no smell so I bring it under my nose. Still no smell. What kind of meat is this? Lifting the bowl to my mouth I take a sip. Still nothing. I take a mouthful. Now I could taste bone, thin, soft, crush. Then a husk of sugar cane get between my teeth. I know it now, is lizard soup: three or four lizards boil up with sugar cane, a cure for cold on the chest or evil spirits. Is almost as bad as wild onion, but one sickly children get used to. I drink and finish just in time to hear Walkback Charlie stomach start to rumble.

'No,' he shout, 'No!'

'Charlie,' Mother Howe say, 'you know the rule!'

'Noooohhh!' Walkback grunt.

'Walkback Charlie, one more sound and you lose.'

Mother Howe take off my blindfold and ask me to stand up. The crowd quiet, like they shock. I get up slow and try to get use to the light.

'Eeeuuuuhhhh! Eeeuuuuhhhhh! Euuuhhhhhh!'

To my left I make out Walkback Charlie bending over his stone. Water pouring from his mouth and nose as if he drowning.

'Take the money,' he say, 'Euuuuh.'

The crowd gasp.

'Euuuuhhh!'

'Charlie?'

'Euuuuuhhhhh!'

'Not eel. Not cook eel. Not cook eel without salt! Euuh!'

'Joel Morgan,' Prince start to chant my name, ' Joel Morgan!'

All of a sudden I feel my feet leave the ground. A man take me by the back and lift me high above his head like a bag of copra. The cheering continue till he put me down. 'Joel Morgan! Joel Morgan! Joel Morgan!'

'Wild onion?' the man ask when I back on my feet, 'you give him wild onion, not true? And then follow up with eel: what you trying to do, kill the man?'

When I steady myself and turn round I see is Cyril. And next to him, Nancy.

Cyril lift me up a second time for the crowd and Nancy do a pretty little dance on both heels like a child glad to see her mother.

'The prize,' Mother Howe say, 'this is the prize, hard money, seventy shillings.'

She hold up the bag for the crowd to see.

'Walkback Charlie,' she say, 'you fight a good fight today. Your stomach long, your stomach strong. You should proud of how long you sit down. But you meet your match today, no need to shame. Once you give of your best you can hold your head to the sky. Joel Morgan, you beat a good man in a fair taste. You are a true mountain man, a real man. Here's your prize. Now, come with me into the house. I want you and Walkback Charlie to tell me the name of all the fruit in the mountain so I could write them down and keep them safe in my Bible.'

'I know how to write,' I tell Mother Howe, 'I can write them down for you.'

'Me too,' Walkback Charlie say, 'and I can count.'

'Nancy and Cyril can read and write too,' I say, 'and they can reckon.'

'Good. Bring them,' Mother Howe say, 'let them come with us. We have a lot of idle children in the village: the four of you can teach them the names of the plants. Before that, you must teach them to read and write.'

I pocket the money and take Nancy left arm. We walk together into the house. Soon we will have some land and a house like this.